NEW
TABOOS

plus...

JOHN SHIRLEY

PM PRESS OUTSPOKEN AUTHORS SERIES

NEW TABOOS

plus

A State of Imprisonment

and

"Why We Need Forty Years of Hell"

and

"Pro Is for Professional"
Outspoken Interview

JOHN SHIRLEY

PM PRESS | 2013

New Taboos
John Shirley © 2013
This edition © 2013 PM Press

Series editor: Terry Bisson

ISBN: 978-1-60486-761-9
LCCN: 2012954998

10 9 8 7 6 5 4 3 2 1

PM Press
P.O. Box 23912
Oakland, CA 94623

Printed in the USA by the Employee Owners of
Thomson-Shore in Dexter Michigan
www.thomsonshore.com

Outsides: John Yates/Stealworks.com
Insides: Jonathan Rowland

CONTENTS

For my wife, Micky, all my love.

A STATE OF IMPRISONMENT

"Minor offenders who cannot pay a fine or fee often find themselves in jail cells. And felony offenders who have completed their prison sentences are often sent back to jail when they cannot pay fees and fines they owe because they could not earn money while locked up. . . . The right to counsel is rarely brought up."
—*The New York Times*, July 13, 2012,
  "Return of the Debtors' Prisons."

1. JANUARY

"I JUST REMEMBER HOW much it hurt when they put the tracker in there. 'This isn't going to hurt,' he says. *Fuck* that! It hurt! But at least *they* used a local . . ."

"You don't need a local, you're numb all over now," Whore Tense said, poising the homemade scalpel over Rudy's ass.

"The fuck I am! A little drunk and slightly opiated— ow! Mother*fucker*, Whore, that *hurts!*"

Rudy was lying naked face down on the bunk; Whore Tense had just started cutting into the fat of Rudy's ass-cheek. "Stop being a baby," she said. "Actually I'm almost there already . . . won't have to cut into muscle . . . sometimes they put it too deep . . . used to be easy to get 'em out when they put 'em right under the skin . . . my first one was in my forearm here, what an ugly bump they made on your skin . . . I still have a scar . . ."

Rudy figured Whore Tense was talking just to keep his mind off the pain. She was a kindly sort.

They were in Rudy's cell, with one of the red imitation-wool blankets hanging over the window in the door to block the cameras and the guard patrol's view, and that was good for a while, anybody checking the monitors would assume they were having sex—which was usually tolerated during certain hours.

Rudy could hear blood tip-tapping onto the floor as she dug the prisoner tracing device out of him. "Don't sound like you're catching that blood," he muttered into the pillow.

"Always miss some. You paid for the clean up, I said I'd clean it up, don't worry about it—"

"Ow! Fuck!"

"Keep your voice down! Hold on now. Almost . . ."

The pain ebbed a bit. There was a clack of instruments—the stolen tweezers probably. Then another jolt of agony . . . and it receded, became a mere throb.

"I got it!" Whore Tense announced breathily, turning it into a squeal.

"Now comes the big fun. Sewing me up . . ."

"No, I got sealant spray and a skin clamp . . ."

She pilfered the wound-closing materials from infirmary storage. Whore Tense's prison job was assistant to the clinician in the pod's infirmary; she was a former RN. She had been Jose Mendoza when she was an RN—when she'd gone about as a *he*. Transgender, she'd gone by Hortense on the outside; in Statewide she got dubbed Whore Tense—with a slight pause between the words—and she went along with the joke.

As Hortense, she'd gotten into debt behind hormone treatments, breast implants, loans to pay for the sex re-assignment—for the operation she never got. She didn't get the hormones here; there were no transgender rights in Statewide. This was Arizona, not California. So Whore Tense had to shave, and lost some body softness. But she got hold of some makeup—made some herself when she had to—and managed her look.

Rudy felt the clamp's pinch and the sealant spray, and hoped it would stay in place. He doubted it.

She cleaned the blood off his ass with Purell wipes, talking to him the while. "Steve'll be here in an hour, what he told me. I got to go to Spanish . . . That boy Doggy going to be there, he sits right in front of me on purpose, I know he likes me . . ."

Whore Tense had been raised by second-generation punk rockers; her dad was Hispanic but he'd never taught her the lingo. She was learning Spanish at a prison class, something about roots. Rumor was that the ed-unit was closing down the Spanish class soon because the lockiffers figured people used it to help them escape into Mexico. But who got anywhere near the border? The state of Arizona was one big privatized prison, so it was just more prison—prison roads, prison buildings, prison fences—between this section and the border. Impossible to know if anyone got through all that. News was censored and Statewide went out of its way to withhold information on the maze of buildings outside pod 775. The ones who were caught in escape attempts went to ARU, the Absconder Recovery Unit, or just never came back at all and the lockiffers made sure you were told they were "shot going over the wire." Or, "the worm crunched 'em."

Mexico. Steve claimed they could get there jumping a robot train, if they could work down the roads ten miles or so. Only, it seemed to Rudy that, chances were, Steve was full of shit. Unless he wasn't.

"Here . . ."

Whore Tense gave him the sippy cup; wincing, he lifted up on his elbows, drank a little of the Vicodin mix. "Ugh."

"Don't drink any more, mess with your head too much. You got to keep it close to clear."

He lay back down, head on his arms, drifting into a dream that wasn't a daydream—but it was half fantasy . . . Mexico . . . a Cantina . . . black-eyed women . . . and then Steve was hissing in his ear.

Rudy opened his eyes. "You're here too soon, hodey."

"You've been laying there more'n an hour."

"I have? Whoa. Stoned."

"Get over it. We got to move."

"About that . . ."

"Don't pussy out on me."

"Man, this shit hurts. How am I going to climb anything?"

"You're going to have some pain while you do it, so fucking what."

"Where's the Ho'tense? What'd she do with the tracker?"

"She took it with her like she's supposed to. It's being passed around the yard. So you'll register as bein' out there. You're committed, Rudy."

"I could take the tracker back."

"And what, Rudy? Stick it in the wound?"

"I don't know . . ."

"Come on, get the fuck up."

Groaning, Rudy pushed himself up, turned to sit on the bunk, wincing, leaning his weight on the unwounded half of his ass. "Ow."

"You don't think *I'm* all about *ow*, too, Rudy? I had it done same as you, hodey-man. I got almost no fat on my ass, either. I'm standing here like a hero."

"You're some hero . . ."

Steve was lean as ropes tied to broomsticks. He had a hollow-cheeked face, deep-set eyes, was missing his front teeth—he always seemed to find a way to get hold of meth—and his arms were spiraled with blue tattoos shaped like barbed wire and devil faces; he had a tuft of beard extending from his pointy chin; his hair was stubble.

Rudy was taller than Steve, and softer, chunkier, hairier. They'd both been working out to prep for the run, but Rudy hadn't made as much progress as he'd hoped.

Slowly, achingly, Rudy got dressed. "I don't know, Steve. Jeezis fuck, hodey, you're five years younger'n me."

"You're not even fifty yet." Soon as Rudy had his orange prison-issue pants on, Steve turned to pull the curtaining blankets off the bars. "Just cowboy the fuck up."

Rudy groaned. "What time is it?"

"Almost zero hour, kumquat." Steve sometimes called people *kumquat,* for no reason anyone could figure out except maybe tweaker humor. "And it's got to be today. It's Sunday, crew's not there and maintenance door is still unlocked. Those pipes'll still be sittin' out. And it's almost dark."

This time of year, it'd get dark pretty damn soon. Someone would be carrying his tracker chip back here, in a few minutes, as prearranged—they'd toss it on his bunk. The tracer program would think he was bunked up . . .

Rudy shook his head but let Steve lead him out of the cell, down the tier, and down the stairs. The pain in his buttock chewed on him as he went, taking a bite with each step.

He glanced at the digital clock over the guard booth. Had to be now. They were both privileged for free passage within area A and B for another half hour . . . and no longer than that.

Keep going. One foot after the other, man.

Rudy was still doped up as he walked mechanically along—only coming to himself when they got to the dig site, where the enclosing walls cornered on the southeast side. The chilly air and a sharp smell of turned, damp earth brought him out of the fog. He thought of graves, and stared into what seemed a grave . . . and then realized it was a trench for a pipe that hadn't yet been laid, just inside the corner.

They were thirty-six-inch-diameter wastewater pipes—Rudy could see the lengths of black plastic pipe stacked up against the cinderblock wall of the interior barricade. There weren't any windows on this side of the prison because they didn't want the inmates to have a view of whatever was past the wall. Which had given rise to a theory . . . that Statewide staff lied about the extent of the prison system. That it wasn't really as big as all Arizona. Rumor had pod 775 only about forty miles from the southern border, and if this was, as some claimed, actually the southern edge of the prison, then it was desert between here and the border. There'd be the occasional drone flying over, out there. But a man would have a chance, if he could jump that robot freight train . . .

Steve was taking several white towels from inside his shirt. He must have stuffed them there when they'd passed through laundry.

"You sure it's blind on this side?" Rudy asked, his tongue thick from the Vicodin.

"Cameras dead over here," Steve said, going over to manhandle a segment of pipe. "Just another thing they're 'working on.' Hey hodey-man, that ever a surprise, something doesn't work around here?"

No, Rudy reflected, that was never a surprise. The McCrue corporation spent as little as possible on prison maintenance. Air conditioning often went out in the summer; heat in the winter. Electricity had blacked out twice in the last three months. Water stopped flowing five or six times a year. McCrue would do maintenance on the auto guards before it'd fix air conditioning, of course. Sometimes the computer-controlled cell doors opened in the middle of the night, for no reason. The gates would immediately close again, because of an emergency over-ride switch.

Wincing when he bent over, Rudy helped drag the six-foot pipe segments out, and lined them up. Steve started hooking them together. The wall was only thirty-three feet high here, not counting the antipersonnel wire. Maybe this would work.

Rudy could see blood blotching through Steve's loose orange trousers, in the back, where his own tracker wound was starting to bleed from all the activity. He felt his own rump—yeah, it was starting to bleed too.

Just power through it, he told himself. *Cowboy up*.

He looked around for guards, living or robotic; didn't see any. Didn't see any inmates, either. This area was supposed to be closed off but a maintenance door had been left unlocked for the sewage pipe crew.

"It's show time, kumquat," Steve said. He took the lower end of the joined-up length of pipe, Rudy took the upper, being taller, and they leaned it in place against the cornering of two walls. The connected pipes sagged a little, but Steve had jammed them together hard. It might hold. Climbing was going to hurt, though.

Cowboy up.

Rudy steadied the lower end of the pipe, as Steve draped the towels around his neck and started to clamber up, like an islander going up a palm tree after a coconut. He used the slight bulge at the joins for handholds. His weight pressed the pipe's lower end into the soft, sandy earth. Rudy kept expecting it to fall apart, but it didn't. Steve didn't weigh as much as he did, though.

It was dark now. When Steve got to the top he was a silhouette against a blue-black sky. His voice was a hoarse whisper. "You coming or not?"

"No way it's gonna hold my weight . . ."

But Steve was up there, hunching on the wall, looking down at him. Waiting. Rudy could see the towels Steve had draped over the antipersonnel wire, to make it climbable. If he turned back now, he'd look weak in the pod, and anyway he'd lie awake nights wondering if he'd lost his chance. He was stuck in the system, here; he wasn't likely to get out for at least fifteen years. Just too much debt, too many rule infractions. They had too much incentive to keep prisoners in.

He wanted to see Lulie. He could arrange for her to come to Mexico . . .

"Are you coming or what, Rudy?"

"I guess." Rudy took a deep breath and started up the pipe, teeth grinding with the pain in his buttocks. After a few yards he felt blood seeping down the back of his leg, and the pipe sagging under his weight. He expected the pipes to fall apart at the joins any second.

Then Steve grabbed him by the collar, and Rudy scrambled the rest of the way up.

He and Steve starting pulling the plastic pipe up, grunting with the weight of it. It stayed together, jammed by their climb. It seemed all one piece of pipe now.

They got it up, then over the wire, and tipped the pipe down. Then lost it. The pipe fell sideways with a wince-making *clunk* to the ground on the other side.

"Shit!" Steve muttered. But he wasn't talking about the pipe. He was standing, holding onto the towel-padded, waist-high razor wire, staring south.

"Shit," Rudy echoed. They had both hoped the rumor was true; that they might see nothing but desert beyond the wall. But prison rumors were usually wrong, and what they saw was a road, a deserted highway. And on the other side of the highway stood another wall. And beyond that, a ways back, was another wall. And beyond that, another prison building rose up . . . and guard towers . . .

Along the highway were alternating streetlamps, leaning in over the tarmac to cast down cones of yellow light . . .

"Shit," Steve said, yet again.

"Yeah. We better go back, man."

Steve shook his head. "We're *locked out* now, dumb shit. The *time*. You know? Locked out of the tier! We got to keep going! That highway has to lead to a way out. We've still got the pipe for the outer walls."

"We're taking the pipe with us down the road?"

"We got no choice, kumquat." Steve was already climbing over the wire, using the towels.

Rudy groaned and followed. "We got no way down . . ."

"Sure we do," said Steve, pausing on the top of the wall, the other side of the wire. "You want some of this before you go?"

He held a little plastic bindle of yellow powder over the wire. Prison meth. Cheap and dirty.

"No, hodey, I don't need a fucking heart attack on top of bleeding to death."

Steve shrugged, grinned, horned some up off a fingernail—and stepped off into space, pulling Rudy with him.

"Shit fuck!" Rudy hissed.

Then he hit the ground. First his feet, then his wounded ass—then he was sliding in sand until he felt dirt clods on his shoulder blades. He jarred to a stop.

He heard Steve chuckle beside him. He thought that was *funny?*

"You hurt, Rudy?"

Rudy was trying to figure that out himself. He turned over, got to his feet, swaying. His feet hurt, maybe one was a little sprained; his ass cheek was bleeding. But nothing seemed broken. "Not much."

"Okay. Let's get the pipe . . ."

They picked up the still-joined pipe, carried it across the highway, half running, Steve taking the lead, like two men with a battering ram. They got it to the ditch—and both of them dived flat in the concrete ditch as headlights came around the curve of the highway ahead.

A car hummed up, and by, headlights coming, taillights going, all in a moment.

They lay there by the pipe, breathing hard, listening. No more cars.

But Rudy thought he heard something else: a whining sound overhead. "You hear a drone?" he whispered.

"Maybe . . . maybe so . . . but they're always whizzin' around the grounds. They're self-guided, these around here, and cheap as shit. They don't see much, especially in the dark."

Rudy doubted they didn't see much, but he didn't argue. He didn't even want to think about the drones. Or the worm.

They stood, and wrestled the pipe up to waist level. Sweat was coming out on Rudy's forehead, burning his eyes.

"Come on, Rudy, goddamnit. We keep going, we find that robot train."

"Don't get ahead of me, you'll pull the pipe apart, Steve."

They trudged along till another set of lights came, this time from behind them. They flattened and the truck rumbled by. They waited till it was around a curve, and then they started off again . . .

There was a sliding, chuffing, metallic grinding sound, from behind . . .

Rudy was afraid to look.

"Fuck, *fuck*," Steve muttered. "They sent out the . . ."

Feeling all clenched up, Rudy dropped his end of the pipe, turned—and looked.

The worm was coming at them like a bad dream. It was about sixty feet long, its body about three feet in radius. It was multi-segmented, its outer skin a mesh tube, nickel-titanium alloy for its muscle—shape-memory alloy expanded and contracted to some internal heat-based prompt. The former IT engineer in Rudy almost admired the worm—unspeakably sophisticated inside, outside it was based on one of the most primitive of organisms. Peristaltically humping, stretching out, humping up, stretching out, it came toward them, in and out of light pole glow, a lamp on its near end for the cameras mounted in the rotating eye cluster.

The worm was a legend at Statewide—but they knew it was real, too. They hadn't known their own pod had one. Staff was secretive about security tech, and the lockiffers just smiled mysteriously when asked about the worm.

Steve had always said, "That creepy smile is just to scare you. They haven't got one here . . ."

But they did. *The drone*, Rudy thought. The drone had seen them, and it had sent the worm.

"Fucking *run!*" Steve shouted, dropping the pipe.

"I don't think we should, man! We gotta surrender! We can't outrun that thing—"

But Steve was already running. Rudy just watched the worm coming—raising his hands over his head so its cameras could take in his surrender. Maybe that would work, maybe not.

The worm turned its segmented metal and plastic snout toward him, reared up, seemed to hesitate a moment. Then it turned, rushed past him, humping with flashing speed, stretching with a whoosh and a *creak*, speeding up . . . catching up with Steve. Its mechanical body blocked Rudy's view as it reared over Steve. One second . . .

Then it slapped down. Steve's scream was short, and sharp.

Rudy waited where he was, keeping his shaking hands over his head. Pretty soon the lockiffer trucks came, and he shut his eyes against the glare of their headlights.

2. JULY

Welcome to Arizona Statewide Prison and Park Access

Underneath those words, in much smaller letters, it said,

A Joint Project of the McCrue Corporation and the State of Arizona.

Faye had abundant time to look at the sign. Her old Chevy was only thirty feet away from it, in a long line of idling cars flanked by other lines of idling cars on the sun-washed highway. They were all waiting to get through the border into Arizona from southeastern California.

Most of the cars had their engines going so they could run the air conditioner in the hot July midmorning sun. Light splashed from the solar collection roofs of the cars. Lots of wasted reflected sunlight, Faye thought.

She sighed. The tedium of the wait was like a stiffened thumb pushing on her forehead. Maybe she shouldn't have come alone, should've brought a photographer at least, someone to talk to. But it had taken months to get permission for her own visit.

She looked at the line of cars to her left, going through one of three entry lanes. They mostly contained people alone in their vehicles, like her. She saw only one family; chubby mother and father, chubby little girl and boy, in a shiny blue hybrid minivan, all of them watching a movie on a popped-up dashboard screen. The rest of the waiting drivers were mostly young to middle-aged men and women, tapping smart phones or staring at the checkpoint; probably here for an interview, hoping to get a job in the penal system.

Stretching, Faye thought about eating some of her fig cookies, and told herself, *No, you're not really hungry, don't eat till you are.* She distracted herself toying with the car radio. Stations blared and receded, crackled and chattered; Spanish-language and Spanglish voices came through. Then she found the public service channel she was looking for: a woman's pleasant voice, her tone like a recording cheerfully welcoming you to a theme park. She sounded as if she might burst into laughter at any moment.

" . . . a warm Arizona welcome to visitors. Visitors to inmates may enter only in Statewide visitors' buses. Non-detention visitors to the state fall into four categories. Tourists are category one, and are required to take the overland express to State and National Parks; category one visitors will need a One Pass. Job applicants are category two and will need a Two Pass. Contractors or prospective contractors on business are category three and will need a Three Pass. Category four is miscellaneous media or retail workers . . ."

That would be me, Faye thought. Miscellaneous media? Maybe I should introduce myself as Miss Alaneous instead of Ms. Adullah.

If she did, they wouldn't laugh. They'd stare. They'd double check her. It was like going through an HSA screening but worse.

". . . and if you're category four, you will need a Four Pass, preprinted with correct scan code."

She patted the folder on the seat beside her, with her print-out Four Pass in it, and all the contingent paperwork.

The line inched forward . . .

About noon she ate the fig cookies and drank some coffee, looking around for a restroom. There was a cinderblock restroom building to the side of the road, but suppose the line moved while she was in the bathroom?

She waited. She thought about her father in Tel Aviv, and wondered if he was going to get his own pass, for over there—a Palestinian Parentage Pass. She remembered Dad watching her sister Weilah die in the Second Ebola Wave.

Dad's face mostly hidden by the white protective mask as he wept soundlessly. He'd left the USA for Tel Aviv, after that, to help his brother in his shop, within a month of Weilah's burial.

She rarely heard from her father anymore. When they talked onscreen he didn't look at her much. She looked too much like Mom, maybe, except for her dark skin, big dark eyes—those were from her father.

Another uncomfortable forty minutes, and she was at the window. "I have a pass, and an appointment," Faye said, smiling. "Faye Adullah."

"May I have your preprinted pass, and your ID?" asked the sturdy black woman in the brown-trimmed yellow uniform. She was looking past Faye, as she spoke, at the horizon; at nothing in particular.

Faye had the folder open on her lap now; she handed over the pass. Why did they say "may I," she wondered, when there was no "may I" about it?

Ten minutes passed, the woman looking at paperwork, scanning codes, gazing into the wafer-thin computer monitor, asking questions that fell between them like abstract shapes in Styrofoam.

"Welcome to Arizona," the woman said, at last, her voice almost inaudible. "After you pass the barrier, drive to slot number five for scan, and then drive directly to your destination."

The scan station at slot five was almost identical to airport TSA. Two white middle-aged men checked the trunk of her car, looking under the spare tire; they ran an instrument over the inside of the car, sniffing for some chemical. They attached a long-distance monitoring device to her car's aerial, one of them explaining that the device would be removed when she left the state.

They rescanned her Four Pass, squinted at her ID, offered her another faint welcome, and sent her through, with a quick warning that drones would be monitoring her car, as they monitored everyone's.

"Well," she said aloud, as she drove onto AzPrisSystem Road 35, "I'm here, Phil. I said I'd get here."

She was in his office, when she said she'd get here. Sitting across from him, two weeks after they'd agree to end their affair.

She reran that wet April morning in her mind; the rain lashing sideways when the wind rose, and it rose as often as a woman takes a breath.

The umbrella hadn't been much use. She was wiping rain from her face and hair when Phil's receptionist told her to go in . . .

• • •

Like Phil, the office was neither large nor small. It was carefully arranged for appearances.

She'd been here before but, after all that had happened between them, the office seemed new to her, its walls and desk festooned with memorabilia of his other life; with pictures of his wife and kids—two sons with curly black hair like Dad, and ornate yarmulkes. There were photos of him interviewing presidents, generals, CEOs. But her eyes kept coming back to the pictures of him with his wife.

Phil was at the window, hands in his pockets, pretending casual interest in the rain. "It's not a heavy rain but it's sneaky," he said, turning toward her. "I see it snuck up on you."

She returned his practiced smile with a weaker one. "Yep."

He motioned toward a chair and sat down behind his desk, leaning back casually as if saying, *The desk isn't between us. We're still friends.*

Were they friends? Faye doubted it. But Phil was the third most influential internet magazine editor in the USA, according to NewsReader.com. He was a fixture at Priority Media, a genuinely powerful corporation, and she was just a freelance journalist. So she kept on smiling.

"So—I read your proposal," Phil said, altering his smile to fit his shrug. "I doubt if I can get Priority to go for it. Everyone knows about this stuff already. Not like there was any shortage of controversy when Arizona became one big privatized prison."

"That was *then*. How much reporting has there been on actual conditions in the state—in the prison?"

"Quite a bit, from what the search engines tell me."

"It was all done in-house, Phil. That's not real reporting."

"You're claiming corporate censorship, spiking, that sort of thing?"

"They don't *have* to censor anything if it comes from in-house. They hire a journalist who does a little segment that he syndicates out, and cable news buys it. They get a pass from any real scrutiny, Phil. I mean, it's a multi-billion-dollar business, and McCrue's financing half of Congress. The company gorges their PACs with cash, it spends millions on lobbyists—and any kind of oversight gets voted down."

Phil nodded mechanically. "Statewide in Arizona, North Louisiana Penal Systems—they're big employers. Not that many flesh and blood jobs around anymore. The jobs give them clout." He swiveled his chair a little, looked out the window again. "And you know, since the ACLU sued ICE over conditions for illegal immigrant prisoners, things have changed. ICE settled, reformed the whole thing."

"That was a *long* time ago and it was only specific to families with children. The basic situation hasn't changed since then—they get money from government for each person in prison, so they're motivated to just *keep* people there any way they can. And privatized prisons are always, *always* motivated to cut corners to maximize profits. Word on the street says it's gotten worse—especially at Statewide . . . Christ, Phil, it's not just Americans and illegal immigrants there! They've brought hundreds of thousands of prisoners in from other countries—they contract with Brazil, Pakistan, the Sudan, even the Chinese. Some of them are political prisoners! And when a prison takes up an entire state . . . how much oversight can there be? How many people do they have to manage? Millions, Phil! What's it *like* for that many people behind bars? I mean—their electrical systems keep failing. Temperatures get up to a hundred-twenty in some of those pods—three people that we know of died in solitary during the heat wave last summer. Who knows what else goes on?"

Phil screwed up his mouth into a twisted cone. "I'll give you that—McCrue runs the place shady. No transparency. They put money before inmate safety. I mean, maybe, if you can get in there on your own, but—you'll want your trip paid for, yeah? You'll want us to provide you with some kind of imprimatur . . . I don't think we can do that, Faye. If you can get there on your own and come back with a good piece . . . documented . . . Then *maybe* . . ."

Faye knew she was supposed to be happy with that and just go away. But it wasn't good enough. She needed this assignment. She was deep in debt, and with the print magazines folded up, she had nowhere else to go. And this story mattered.

She had just one card left to play. "Phil—you *have the authority* to assign this! You *owe* me one. Just one! I really *need* this . . ."

He looked at her, his shoulders stiffening, eyes narrowed. The wreckage of their intimacy was there in the room with them. His promises. *Yes, I'll divorce Miriam. Give me time, Faye. Another year . . .*

And his betrayals. *Can't do it. It would wreck my life, Faye. My career.*

Finally, Phil exhaled noisily through his nose. "Okay. Okay, fine."

• • •

Faye had three more hurdles after the border, each human hurdle closely inspecting her Four Pass: first, another checkpoint; next, a meeting with one of Statewide's staff attorneys, a buff, lisping man named Biggle, who tried to get her to sign a nondisclosure agreement even after admitting that it was a strange thing to ask of a journalist. But when she referenced the ACLU—which had been making a comeback, after being almost nonfunctional following the countersuits of 2025 and 2026—he got a resigned look on his face and went to make some phone calls. When he came back, he sighed and said, "Well, I can let you go to *select* pods . . . One, anyhow. Pod Seven-seventy-five."

The third hurdle was McCrue's Statewide media liaison—a tall, vulpine blond woman named Rita Burse.

"They've asked me to be your guide around pod seven-seventy-five," she said, looming over Faye in the warden's reception room. Burse had a beakish nose, small lips, and her blue eyes seemed oddly far apart. Her accent was Southwest; her suit dress was light blue tweed; the color of her pumps matched the dress. She had an e-board tucked against her lapels.

"Will I see the warden, today?" Faye asked, glancing at his office door. The small plastic sign on the door said *Ervin Holmes, Warden.*

"Warden Holmes is on vacation," Burse said, looking at Faye's laptop case. "We'll have to inspect your laptop for webcams—we can't allow those here at all, or any other photography."

"*No* photography? I'm a journalist, Ms. Burse."

"Do please call me Rita. Um, we provide photos, we have a set for every pod. You can take some pictures from of the building from the parking lot, if you like . . ."

"I can see how this is going to go, Rita."

"I beg your pardon?"

"Doesn't matter, really," Faye said, adding dryly, "Long as I don't have to wear a blindfold."

They wouldn't let me take photographs of the interior of the pod might be a good opening line for the article, Faye thought.

"Here's your badge," Rita said, handing her a badge with her photo on it, plus her name and a sensor chip.

"Where do we start?" Faye asked, clipping the badge to her jacket. "Could I see a map of the facility? I mean—of seven-seventy-five."

"That . . . no. I didn't get an authorization for that. Most of the facilities have pretty much the same layout." The door to the corridor opened and a bulky, uniformed man came in. "Here's Samuel. He's our Special Officer . . ."

The burly shaven-bald guard was swag-bellied but wide-shouldered. The flat-black and yellow uniform didn't fit him properly—around the middle and the shoulders it seemed small; it seemed a little too long in the legs, wrinkling over his shiny black shoes. His ID badge said, *Samuel Gull, Cust. Spec, SpecOff.* He wore a glossy black belt with a variety of cryptic items holstered in it.

The guard stepped closer to Faye, towering over her, smiling thinly. His lower jaw stuck out a little more than his upper. She saw that he had a headset plug in his ear, with a little projection snaking from it to the corner of his mouth.

What a couple you two would make, Faye thought, looking back and forth between Rita and Gull. *Or maybe you do . . .*

"Samuel?" Rita said. "This is Faye Adullah."

Faye thought there might be a flicker of suspicion in his eyes at the Arab last name.

She stuck out her hand; his enormous hand was like sandpaper on hers. "Welcome to McCrue Statewide," he said. He had a voice like a tuba.

"Samuel, we're going to Crafts and Training One, first," Rita said.

"Yes ma'am. Right this way . . ."

It was a long walk. The door to the corridor was the first of six doors—or was it seven? Faye thought she might've lost count.

Two of the doors were within a few paces of one another, both of those were metal, with wired glass panes, and both opened by "buzzing in" after inspection by someone on the other side of the security camera.

Gull led the way down a long corridor to another door, his shoes squeaking as he walked. He waved to someone on the other side, held the buzzing door open . . .

They clip-clopped through more passages, more doors, walked down a narrow side corridor. The place looked clean, the walls painted peach, here; dun in other places. The floors were pale green. A middle-aged Hispanic trustee with slicked-back hair and a small goatee was kneeling beside a floor-cleaning machine, a kind of wet vacuum cleaner, trying to clear a jam. He wore a one-piece orange uniform, and a white plastic ID on a thong around his neck.

Gull glanced at the trustee, and they strode on. The trustee looked up at Faye as she slipped by, surprise widening his eyes. Faye felt him watching as they went through another door . . .

● ● ●

The Craft and Training Unit consisted of seventeen male inmates in orange jumpsuits, working around tables in a brightly lit wire-windowed room; they were almost evenly divided between Hispanic, white, and black—and one had a Sikh's turban and beard. The inmates barely glanced up when Faye followed Samuel and Rita in. Unlike the trustee in the corridor, they didn't seem surprised to see her.

They knew we were coming, Faye decided. *They were briefed.*

A sleek, wheeled autoguard stood in the corner, silently watching. It was five feet high, black and white, its body smoothly prow-shaped, its head like a smaller version of its body, a green light glowing from its black-glass view pane. There were two lights on either side of its body, one red and one blue, like the lights on police cars, unlit in the absence of crisis; between the lights was a grid for its computer voice—and for a siren. A panel under the grid would open, she knew, to emit crowd control gases. The robot's head turned smoothly and took the visitors in; she assumed it was processing the signals from their badges. It swiveled back to the prisoners.

A couple of much-tattooed white inmates, heads shaved, glanced up as she approached their table, smiling at her. They looked at her legs, and then back at their craft construction: they were working with intricate wooden parts, connected by screws and nuts and bolts, all made of wood. There was no need for screwdrivers, for saws, for any tool but a small wrench of light plastic. She looked around and saw everyone was working with the same materials, but some were building miniature houses, some constructing little cars—rather well-realized cars—and there were three sculptures of human shapes, including one that was clearly female but not embarrassingly so.

"This is a hand-skills class," Rita said. "Advanced. They don't need an instructor. It preps their motor skills so they can do factory assembling later."

Faye looked inquiringly at Gull. "Can I talk to some of them?" He looked, in turn, at Rita, who gestured grandly at a table. The gesture said, *Of course*—but Faye suspected these would be the only prisoners she was allowed to talk to.

She stepped up to a prisoner at the end of the nearest table. "Hi, I'm Faye," she said to him. "I'm a journalist from Priority Media."

"Derreck," he said, glancing up. He had a small gray mustache; several little blue teardrops were tattooed at the corner of each eye. Despite the teardrops, he seemed cheerful.

"Can I look at your model car?" Faye asked.

"Sure, check it out!" He held it out to her. "It's mostly finished . . ."

It was about fifteen inches long, a well-proportioned mockup of a convertible. "It's amazing all the detail you can get in with those prefab parts, Derreck . . ."

He nodded, gazing critically at the car. "Yeah, but there's so many kind of parts, see, you get good at making lot of different things with 'em . . ."

He took the car back, looking up at her for a lingering moment; she was aware that he was taking in her figure, though it wasn't much in evidence. Then he looked fixedly back at the car.

"What's your feeling about McCrue Statewide, Derreck?"

He shot a quick look at Rita. She looked at him with raised eyebrows. *Go on, answer her.*

"Well, it's *prison*," Derreck said, nervously removing a wheel and refastening it onto an axle. "No one's thrilled to be in one. I mean—prison is prison. All pretty alike."

"Are they? Some privatized prisons have whole families in them. Seen anything like that?"

"Naw, this isn't that kind. They do keep some peeps for Immigration here, in Sub12, but not like that."

"Nothing to complain about?"

He shrugged. "Like to have more variety in the food. More commissary stuff. Lights go out sometimes when you're trying to go to the head."

Rita checked her watch. "Shall we visit the meals department?"

• • •

Several bored inmates were drinking coffee in a small room lined with white and chrome appliances.

Faye, Gull, and Rita were standing near a gray metal door with *Subpod 17* stenciled under the wired window. She could see only corridor through the window—and the trustee she'd seen earlier, running his wet vacuum over the floor. Had he followed them here, somehow?

She'd expected a big cafeteria space, an industrial-sized kitchen. But meals was a just a series of distribution counters, that opened in various parts of the prison pod at mealtimes, closed with steel shutters the rest of the time. There were no cooks, just a few personnel who did the microwaving. The food was prefab, each meal in its Styrofoam tray, brought to the pod on trucks once a week.

The breakfasts were all the same, except on Sundays when they added pancakes; there were seven lunches and suppers, one for Monday, one for Tuesday . . .

"It's true that the food is . . . kind of repetitive," Rita said. "We're working on offering more variety. But it's nutritious, sprayed with vitamins, everything they need. Would you like to try today's lunch? We have meat loaf, or, if you prefer, veggie loaf. It's all kosher."

"No thanks. Just the coffee . . ."

"Coffee's not bad, don't you think?"

"No. Not bad." It wasn't bad. It wasn't good. It wasn't important.

"Shall we go to the printers?" Rita suggested.

They went. Another long passage through many doors took them to a big hangar-like room where men in orange jumpsuits guided blocks of basic production plastic into 3-D printers. The inmates looked into monitors, made adjustments on a computer screen, and talked softly under the watchful eyes of four autoguards. A variety of car parts, printed three-dimensionally, were shunted out of the printer; workers checked them for symmetry and defects, then stacked them.

"Those printers can make any shape," Faye murmured. "Isn't that kind of dangerous? Can't they make weapons?"

"What the printers can make is preprogrammed. The prisoners can't program them here, not at all. This stuff can't be hacked. Every last piece is closely monitored. Prisoners absolutely cannot make contraband forms. If anything's missing, the mechanism knows it right away from the weight differential."

Faye pointed to the odor marked *Subpod 17.* "What's through there?" she asked Gull.

"That's high-security," he said, glancing at Rita.

"Can we have a look through it?"

Rita slowly shook her head. "It's not safe."

"That's kind of a contradiction in terms, high-security that's not safe, isn't it?"

"Not if you know prisons," Rita said, giving her a look of watered-down contempt.

"That's just why I'm here," Faye said. "Because I *don't* know them—particularly this style of prison. This is the biggest prison in the world. It covers an entire state. I really need to be able to see it pretty extensively to get a sense . . ."

Rita gave her a pitying frown. "It doesn't actually cover the whole state. Arizona is still . . . Arizona."

"Statewide covers a little more than eighty percent of the state of Arizona," Faye said. "That's more than three-fourths of the state covered with thousands of buildings like this one . . ."

"Ms. Adullah. We can show you medium-security cell tiers, and one of the yards, and that will have to be it. You could spend months trying to see even half of Statewide—And you'd see the same thing over and over, though some pods contain men, some contain women—"

The lights went out. All of them, just like that.

There was a *click* to Faye's left, and a noise she'd only been peripherally aware of till now receded: the humming from the 3-D printers faded; the prisoners muttered . . .

A few whirling lights went on, shining from the autoguards across the room. "Stay in place until power is restored," said a man's firm voice, emanating from one of the robots. It was a deep, commanding, very natural-sounding voice but entirely synthetic. "Stay in place . . ."

The lights cut back to almost no illumination as the robots trundled behind machinery, establishing that the prisoners were staying immobile.

"*Samuel?*" Rita's voice was taut with annoyance and serrated with fear. "Can you get a timetable on power restoration?"

"Yes, ma'am, I'm hearing it right now. They're telling me . . . they're not sure. They're not sure what's happened."

Faye could feel cool air drifting over her from the left. That click must have been a door opening, unlocked by the electronic disruption.

You wanted your chance, she thought. *Here it is. You can tell them you got lost in the dark . . .*

No. Really stupid to do that. But . . .

There was no other way to find out . . .

Don't do this, Faye.

But operating on sheer will power, Faye turned, hands outstretched, and felt her way along, till she got to the frame of the doorway. The metal door was standing slightly open. Still mostly blind, she felt her way through the door and into the corridor that led to Subpod 17. She could hear Gull talking to someone behind her . . .

I should turn back.

Then a hand closed over her wrist. It was a hand with a sweaty palm, smaller than Gull's. She assumed it was Rita's. The hand tugged on her and she went with it, suddenly not wanting to be in the dark in this big room with all those inmates. "Rita? That you?"

"No." A man's voice from the darkness. A light, Hispanically accented voice. Not Gull. "You okay. You came to see, so I take you."

"I can't see *anything*. I should go back . . ."

But she let herself be drawn through another doorway. Was it curiosity, ambition, opportunism . . . a desire to get to the truth . . . She wasn't sure.

Go back, you fool.

Then a light came on just ahead—a flashlight, the beam angling downward, the glow shining upward enough to show her the man holding the light.

"This is her, the reporter," said the man who had her wrist.

He let go of her, and she looked back and forth between them. The man she'd followed was the trustee she'd seen working on the floors. The other man seemed slightly Asian, his skin cocoa, his features mostly Caucasian, his hair straight and smooth.

"My name's Rudy," he said. "Welcome to ARU."

She licked her lips. Her mouth was so dry. She was alone with two prisoners. "Um—ARU?"

"Absconder Recovery Unit. A punishment unit, if you've been naughty. I've been here since I tried to escape." He turned to the trustee. "Carlos, man—did you shut that door behind her?"

"Yeah, hodey. But they'll find her when the cameras come back on."

"What happened to the lights?" she asked, for something to say. Trying to decide if she should turn around and bolt back down the hall.

Rudy shrugged. "Shitty system. It's easy to overload it, get a surge going that shuts it down. If we talk to a trustee in heating and air conditioning—they can do it."

Carlos hooked a thumb at Rudy. "Him, he was an engineer."

"Computer engineer, on the outside," Rudy said. "What the fuck, Carlos, we got to show her at least Unit 18, before they find her."

Carlos nodded. "Come on. Lights out for only a few minutes more."

She followed the swinging flashlight and the two men along a walkway; to her left was a wall, to her right were doors, with wired glass windows in them. Faces appeared at the windows to watch, looking ghostly in the shifting, indirect light. Someone shouted at her from a door. She hurried to catch up with Carlos and Rudy.

They reached the end of the tier, and Carlos tried the door. "Still unlocked!"

"How about the doors to the outside world?" Faye asked.

Rudy chuckled. "Separate circuits. Plus there are autoguards, there are drones, there's the worm, more walls, more buildings, just more and more and more, lady."

"Electric fences, you go far enough," Carlos said, leading the way through the door. "Couple of miles out from here. First touch on gives you a little jolt, makes you jump back. Try again, lethal jolt."

That reminded her of something she'd read, somewhere, in her research. "*Privatized prisons are so badly built and so inefficiently run they have to be especially harsh to keep prisoners in.*"

They were in a different style of cellblock now. There were bars instead of the wired-window doors. "This is Sub18," Rudy said. "Part of an old jail. They built the prison around it. They like to have the view into the cells from the walk, here . . ."

There were women in the cells, Faye saw; two women in each. They all seemed to be cringing back away from the flashlight as it went by. Most of them were Hispanic; she saw two black and one white woman. All of them were fairly young. They wore prison orange shifts.

"I was told there were no women prisoners in this pod," Faye said, barely aware she'd said it out loud.

"Not any on the books," Rudy said.

"I should talk to them." For a moment she found she couldn't quite speak, then she asked, "Rudy—is this what . . . Is it . . ."

"Yeah, Rudy said. "These women are kept here for people to use. Not for other prisoners. I mean, they're here for big shots, and prison personnel. When they get old enough they get harvested . . . Oh *fuck!*"

The lights were going on, starting down the tier, flick flash flick flash, as if stalking down the hallway toward them. Faye blinked in the sudden blaze of light.

Rudy looked around, eyes widening. "Shit—Carlos we got to get back before . . ."

Too late. The autoguards were coming from both ends of the cellblock. Behind one of the autoguards came Rita and Gull staring coldly at Faye as they marched toward her. They seemed quite confident behind the rolling, flashing machines.

"*Do not move*," the autoguards said simultaneously. "*Remain exactly where you are.*"

• • •

Faye sat in the warden's office, across from his desk, her wrists cuffed in front of her. The hand cuffs were linked by a long shiny steel chain to ankle restraints. She wore a prison ID badge on a thong around her neck. She was still in shock, feeling unreal.

She was sitting in the warden's office, across from the desk. Sitting at the desk, silent and nervous, was a pale, nearly chinless man in his midsixties, wearing a white shirt and tie, with a badge that said, *Howard Skaffel, Assistant Warden*. Rita stood beside him, her arms crossed against her chest, face expressionless. Gull was waiting just outside the door. Faye could hear him shift his weight out there from time to time.

"Are you a Muslim, Faye?" Rita asked.

She'd called her Ms. Adullah before. Now she'd switched to that condescending use of the first name that people in authority chose when they were treating you like a bad child.

Just get through this. They can't do this for long. Eventually they have to let you go. They're just trying to scare you.

"A Muslim?"

"Your father was Muslim."

"It's not an ethnicity. It's a religion. I'm not a believer."

"You're half Palestinian."

"I'm partly Arab, if that's what you mean. My mother was Italian American. Is this some kind of Homeland Security question? I had to be completely cleared before they let me in here, you know. You have my Four Pass. Look at it again."

"People make mistakes in granting clearances," Skaffel said, looking at the ceiling. The assistant warden hadn't looked directly at her the whole time she was here. He pursed his mouth. For the first time he looked at her— only momentarily. Then he looked down at the papers on his desk. "We have a court order here, based on your trespassing, and the Probation Collections review of your debts. You're thirty-two thousand dollars in debt, young lady."

She snorted. "So? Who isn't, who went to college? I missed a couple of payments when the *Trib* folded, true, but . . ."

"You should've discussed that with Debt Court."

"I did! I was given an extension."

He glanced up at her and tapped the paper. "Probationary only. Your probation has been revoked. PCI took your case to Judge Gipps this morning."

"This is absurd. I want to speak with my lawyer!"

"You waived that right," Rita said softly.

"What? When?"

"We have the paperwork."

"I never signed any such thing."

Rita shrugged. "We have your signature."

"That's not my signature and you know it. You don't want me to talk about what I saw in Subpod 18—"

"If you continue shouting," Skaffel said, looking at his hands, "I'll have Samuel take you to Unprivileged Custody. You won't like UnCus."

Had she been shouting? Faye realized she had. She controlled her tone. "Just get me a lawyer. I'm a journalist. I was sent here by one of the country's biggest media companies. They're not going to let this . . ."

"Do you *suppose*," Skaffel said, studying his fingernails, "that this is, what, 1975? We're in touch with Priority Media. They deny giving you permission to use their name here."

"That's not true. You saw my paperwork!"

"Faked. That little bit of fraud is a felony."

"I don't believe any of this. Put someone from Priority on the speaker phone."

Skaffel ignored that. "We have found that you're a debt felon. The Privatization Act of 2021 gives us the right to arrest and incarcerate you until you've served your term or paid your debt—"

Nothing to lose.

"You know what I think, Assistant Warden Skaffel?" Faye said, leaning forward to catch his eye. "I think you're really, deeply ashamed of what I saw in Subpod 18—"

"Gull!" Skaffel bellowed, standing so suddenly his chair pitched over behind him.

The door opened, Gull creaked into the room in his squeaky shoes. "Yes sir?"

Skaffel's voice was a hiss now. "Take this inmate to UnCus."

"I'm a journalist, not an inmate and you know it!"

Then she was spun about, her arm painfully wrenched, and pushed through the open door . . .

An autoguard was waiting outside, its eyeless face scanning her.

She was afraid of the autoguards. She let Gull and the autoguard shuffle her off, the chains clinking, through corridors and glass-wired metal doors, another corridor to a freight elevator where she stood trembling between the robot and the man as the wide gray box descended.

Then she was escorted along a damp corridor in a basement to a door with a little window, and into a room where the light never went out, and there was a foam rubber pad on a bench built into the wall . . . a seatless toilet . . .

She tried to talk to Gull as he took off the cuffs. "You can help yourself by reporting this, now, to Priority Media, and to the Justice Department, Samuel . . ."

"Breakfast is at seven," he said, leaving the little room. The lock clicked sharply, making a definitive statement.

3. SEPTEMBER

Phil. It had to be Phil.

He denied I was on assignment from Priority. He must have. But why?

Faye turned over on her bunk, facing the wall.

He misunderstood. Thought I was threatening him.

She picked at a paint bubble on the concrete wall and shivered. The chills were back. The place where they'd shot her in the rump with the tracker burned. She suspected the wound might've become infected. She hadn't submitted to the tracker without fighting. They'd had to hold her down. She didn't remember an alcohol swab.

He seduced me and dumped me and yes I guilted him a little to get the assignment. But I didn't threaten him.

She looked up at the scratched-in graffiti on the wall. "I am a jewl," it said. "I sparkle like a jewl. I'm a jewl buried underground."

Buried underground. *Phil thought I was going to tell his wife. Thought there'd be a divorce and he'd lose custody of his boys. So he set me up. Put me in here.*

She heard the scrape of the tray coming through the slot in the door. She could smell the food. It made her feel sick to smell it. She'd stopped eating a while ago. Food just came up if she ate.

She'd stopped trying to talk to the guards, too. Stopped demanding her phone call, stopped demanding a lawyer. Demands got her no response, none. Which was a response itself.

Someone will come looking for me . . .

But they probably wouldn't. She had no siblings, no boyfriend, no close friends who'd search for her. *Maybe I can get Phil a message. Tell him I didn't mean what he thought. All is forgiven. Just get me out. He knows people.*

The light flickered.

She looked up at the caged bulb, hoping for a power outage. It was burning steadily. She'd tried to break it already once but it was out of reach

She looked back at the paint bubble, and widened it a little, working at its edges with her fingernail, concentrating.

The light flickered.

She looked quickly up at it.

It wasn't flickering.

Phil. It must've been him. Or . . .

The light.

She looked up at it. It burned steadily.

Faye closed her eyes, and put her arm over her face. She could smell herself. She'd stopped washing a few days earlier. Maybe a week.

She breathed in her own smell. It was an interesting smell.

She felt the chills again . . .

• • •

"Girl, you got to learn how to do time in solitary."

The voice was womanly but it seemed to lilt a bit too much. Faye felt a sponge on her neck.

"How's that feel?" the voice fluted.

Faye opened her eyes. She was lying on her back, looking up at a man who wore some kind of makeup around his brown eyes; eyeliner and blue shadow. He was smiling down at her, and it was the first genuine smile she'd seen since she'd come across the border into Arizona Statewide. He was dark-skinned, lanky, with big hands. He had his black hair tied up in a bun on top of his head. He wore an orange jumpsuit, and a trustee badge.

"Look at you, finally waking your ass up!" the man said.

Faye looked around. She was in a hospital bed, wearing a clean prison shift, in an infirmary of some kind, not large, with white walls. Light green curtains partially blocked off her area. She shifted on the bed and felt a tug at her right arm, saw an IV needle attached to a soft plastic bottle hung on a thin metal pole. A bubble was moving slowly up the IV tube, as if it were escaping.

She tried to move her left arm but it was cuffed to a rail running along the bedframe. Still in prison. "How long have I been here?"

"'Bout two days, girlfriend. I'm Hortense."

"Faye."

"Oh I know, I seen your charts. You had an infection where they shot you with the tracker. Your fever's way down, though."

"I'm hungry."

"I'll bring you some soup. Here, let me adjust the bed, get you sitting up . . ."

Faye waited, still sleepy, dazed, the five-minute wait seeming more like an hour, before Hortense bustled back to her, working extra girlishness into her walk. At some point, Faye had started thinking of the man as a woman.

"See, in solitary," Hortense was saying, sitting the Styrofoam bowl of yellow-orange soup on the little steel table beside the bed, "you got to find a way to stay busy. You can exercise and make up poems, find something to do, keep your head on straight. Here . . ."

She carefully lifted a spoonful of the soup to Faye's mouth. It tasted of pumpkin and beans; delicious, probably because she was so hungry.

"Even the soup wears orange here," Faye said.

Hortense laughed.

"I can feed myself."

"Girl, let me finish giving you this bowl, I got to make myself seem useful in here. You know what, I made up poems in UnCus—I put one on the wall, about how I felt like a jewel."

"Oh! That was my cell!"

"Oh yeah?"

"Yes, your poem . . . kept me company." It seemed like the right thing to say.

Hortense was pleased. "They give you anything to write with?"

"No. They didn't want to encourage anything like journalism."

Hortense chuckled, gave her some more soup, and then became grave. "The guards . . . the human guards? You can trade stuff, you know. You're not someone who'd think of it, right off. But most likely you will later."

"Trade? . . . Oh."

"You make the offer, they come in, and cuff you to a pipe on back of the toilet and . . . it's usually a blow job. That might get you a book. Magazines. First time he brought me some fishing magazines! What I want with fishing magazines? I wanted *InFashion*."

"You sound like you heard something about me—you knew I was in Unprivileged Custody. Heard anything else?"

"You going to ask me if I heard about your case?" Hortense shook her head. "Just heard a story they were really mad at you and you were a reporter. Girl reporter! Seems like a hard job. I get out, I'm going to go back to haircutting school."

"You know when they're letting you out?"

"I'm a short-timer, girl. Four weeks and four days—If I don't mess up. Even a little screw up is bad. They find an excuse to keep you, they will. Some people . . . my friend Rudy, he and Steve messed up big. They'll never let him out."

"They have to let him out sometime if they're not convicted of murder . . ."

Hortense shook her head sadly.

"No, girl, they *don't* have to. This isn't government, this is corporation stuff. They make their own rules here. You got to twist yourself around like a rubber band, stretch yourself into any shape they want. They punish people in here. They . . . Well, I found my way. That's all." She extended the plastic spoon. "You eat up now."

Faye swallowed some more soup. "How about someone like me?"

Hortense shrugged, and seemed to be considering a reassuring response.

"For real, Hortense. What do you think'll happen to me here?"

"For *real?* I heard you were going to *tell* on them. About Sub 18, all that other. I never heard of *anyone* reporting on them anything they didn't want said. I don't know what they're going to do with you. I surely do not. But they're not going to let you go. The McCrue company'd lose too much money, girl."

4. OCTOBER

"Absconder unit for someone like you," Rudy was saying, "is probably on the way to somewhere else. Maybe psyche eval, remand to the crazy pod. Maybe Sub 18."

"I'm *not* staying in prison," Faye said firmly. "I'm . . ." An autoguard trundled by on its wheels, watching them without turning its plastic and metal head, and she finished lamely, "I'm . . . just not."

She was outside—but inside too. They were each allowed one hour in the outdoor exercise cages which extended out from the back of absconder unit—they were steel mesh open-air pens with a gap of about five feet between them. It felt zoolike. Several human guards stood together, talking, across the courtyard area from her. *Lockiffers*, the prisoners called them. But being out here where she could see sky and sun was an enormous relief. Faye looked up at a wispy cloud, elegantly attenuated, startlingly white against the blue sky. She couldn't remember looking at a cloud so closely before—not since childhood. Or seeing a sky quite so perfectly turquoise-colored.

The breeze was coming from the south, wending its way between buildings. She could smell sage, and minerals. She could glimpse other prisoners in other cages beyond Rudy. They were all men.

"Rudy—how come they're keeping me here, where I'm the only woman? Letting me come outside like this . . . Why don't they put me in some woman's population?"

She thought she knew the answer. Hortense had hinted at it. She was hoping Rudy had another response.

He started to say something, then broke off. A moment later he shrugged and said, "One thing, you got sick. They got to get you well. So. Coming out here helps. And . . ." He broke off again, as someone walked up to the cages, shoes squeaking.

It was Gull, hands in his jacket pockets. He ignored Rudy and paused near Faye's fence, his gaze roaming freely over her. He had a look of speculation on his face. "You have ten minutes more out here," he told her, before strolling on.

She thought about calling him back just to once more demand a lawyer, or at least the phone call she'd never gotten. But they just shrugged, if they reacted at all, when she asked for those things. There was one possibility, something as wispy as that cloud. It probably wouldn't work.

Don't think like that. It has to work.

Rudy watched Gull till he was out of earshot. "Never see that guy around here," he said, in a low voice. "He seems to be keeping you under some kind of personal surveillance."

Faye wondered about Phil. Was this really all down to him? All this time, no one looking for her? It had to be his doing. He just hadn't seemed like that kind of person. He was no saint. But still . . .

Faye looked to see where the autoguards and the lockiffers were. None of them were close by. "Rudy . . ." She turned her back on the courtyard, making her voice as low as she could and still be heard by him. "There have to be cell phones in here somewhere. The prisoners have to . . ."

He shook his head. "Cell phones are bigtime contraband," he said glumly. "Used to be people keistered them in. But you can't keister anything now—they got machines that look right through you. I haven't seen a cell phone in years, except when the guards use them—and even they aren't supposed to use them except in emergencies. No. Got to think of something else."

• • •

Gull came into her cell right after breakfast the next morning; a stocky black guard with a heavy belly and yellowed eyes came with him, the man silent, except occasionally humming tunelessly to himself. The black guard had no identification badge on, but he carried a set of handcuffs loosely in his hands. Both men had gas masks hanging loosely around their necks, in case of need. Outside the cell an autoguard waited, eerily silent, somehow radiating alertness. Faye could see its chest panel was open; inside the panel was a row of nozzles. "Be careful," Rudy called, from across the hallway. He was shouting through the hole in the door. "They got that panel open, they're full on Dalek! They'll spray you with 'ouch'!"

He'd told her about "ouch"—a gas that suffused your lungs with burning agony once you breathed it in. It paralyzed you with pain. He'd told her about the worm, too, and what had happened to Steve. She wasn't eager to fight with robots.

"What do you want, Gull?" she asked.

"We're moving you," he said.

"For the record, I'm demanding a phone call and a lawyer, *again*, neither of which I've ever had. I demand them right now! I assume that robot records everything."

"Not everything," Gull said blandly. "Come on."

The black lockiffer made the bored, twirling gesture with his hand that meant turn around.

The inside of Faye's mouth felt desiccated; her heart was pounding. She looked at the black guard, trying to catch his eye. "What's your name?" she asked.

He didn't look directly at her. Like Skaffel. He made the twirling gesture again.

"Turn around *now*," Gull said. "Autoguard, be ready."

Faye turned slowly around and put her hands together behind her back. She felt the cuffs pinch down, closing cold on her wrists; she felt the discomfort in her shoulders. It was all becoming familiar.

"Turn around," Gull said. "Go out the door. Turn right, ahead of the autoguard, take one step and then stop."

Maybe this is all drama to scare me. Maybe this time they're letting me go.

She'd had that same thought many times before.

Now she walked out of the open cell door, turned right, took a step, and stopped. She saw a man looking at her from another cell. It was the trustee, Carlos. He was stuck in ACU because he'd been caught leading her to Subpod 18.

He nodded to her, with no bitterness in his face. She nodded back.

She heard Gull squeaking up behind her. "Go ahead, on down the hall," he said.

Faye walked on, her knees weak. The ACU door clicked open ahead of her, directed by the robot. She walked through, down a short corridor. Another door clicked open. She was in Subpod 18. The walkway stretched ahead of her, concrete and iron on the left, old-fashioned barred cells on the right. But now she was seeing it in full light. She heard women talking to one another, one of them laughing, another crying, another calling someone a bitch hag, "just a fucking bitch hag, just a . . ." Bitch hag, over and over. They passed a cell where a black woman said something to her in a Jamaican patois too thick to understand.

The guards were fulsome presences behind Faye. Someone hissed a warning at their approach, and the women's voices quieted.

Then she came to an open cell.

"Enter the cell," said Gull.

Feeling like she was sleepwalking, Faye stepped into the cell. The black guard slid the barred door shut behind her.

"Take a step back, toward the bars," Gull said.

She did. The other guard reached through, unlocked her cuffs, and took them. She straightened her arms and stretched.

"Inmate Gloria Munoz, dinner is in two hours," Gull said. "There'll be a consultation after dinner."

Faye turned to see who Gull was talking to. He was looking straight at her. There was just the suggestion of a smile on his face. The black guard was walking away; the autoguard was waiting quietly, beside Gull.

"What did you say?" Faye asked.

"Gloria Munoz, dinner is in—"

"*What?*"

A woman she couldn't see in the cell to her right said, "Bitch, that your name, just shut up! You Gloria now!"

Some of the women laughed. One of them sobbed.

"You're not going to pull that bullshit," Faye said, her voice cracking. She turned to the robot. "You record this! My name is Faye Adullah, my address is—"

"It's not recording now," Gull interrupted. "You're wasting your breath. Here, look."

He unclipped an electronic wand from his belt. One end of the wand held a sensor; the other end had a little screen, like a smartphone. He pointed the sensor end at her. "Reading your tracker now, and . . . Look."

He held it so she could see the screen. She saw her face on the screen, a miniaturized mug shot. She saw a number under the face, and under that, the name, *Gloria Munoz.*

"I don't even look the part," she said hoarsely.

"Guatemalan, illegal immigrant," he said. "Extensive criminal record. Gloria Munoz. Get used to it."

She looked him in the eyes and said in a low, flat voice, "I'm not going to get used to it."

He returned the wand to his belt, and walked past the autoguard. It remained behind, for a long moment, seeming to watch her.

A woman laughed. A woman sobbed.

The robot rolled away.

• • •

Faye made herself eat part of her dinner, some kind of meat and cheese quesadilla from a package. She washed it down with water from her sink. She went to the toilet, tried to pee. Couldn't, though it felt like she needed to.

She went to the bunk and lay down. Her stomach burbled.

Gloria Munoz. Get used to it.

She picked at a paint bubble on the wall.

I should try to talk to the other girls . . .

Later. There would be time. She just felt too limp. She felt like a fly badly swatted. Alive but broken, buzzing to itself as it slowly died. *Buzzzzz.*

Faye closed her eyes. The women's voices seemed to merge into the buzzing . . . After a while the corridor lights went down. They didn't go out completely. The women got quieter. She heard footsteps, and a cell door opening, voices she couldn't understand. She turned to look as someone walked by. It was the Jamaican woman, escorted by the heavy black guard, and a robot. She had her hands cuffed behind her.

"She going to the berdwar," one of the women said, down the hall a little.

Berdwar? *Boudoir.* Rudy had mentioned a special cell . . .

Faye turned over on the bunk and picked at the paint bubble. Voices echoed down the hall, unintelligible. Perhaps half an hour passed. *The berdwar.*

Faye closed her eyes.

Don't let them do this. Even if you have to kill yourself.

The bunk was old-style. It had metal-mesh under, that made sounds like a crow when she shifted. She might be able to unwind some of that mesh, sharpen it somehow, and tear her wrists up. Better to bleed to death than to . . .

"Gloria Munoz."

Just ignore it. Don't respond to that name.

The cell door clicked. She turned to see who was coming in.

"Gloria . . ." Gull's voice.

"My name is Faye Adullah."

He seemed to have come alone, with not even an autoguard. He licked his lips, looking unusually self-conscious, his arms gangling at his sides. He glanced behind him, then went to the wall beside her, leaned against it, arms crossed over his chest, and spoke in a low voice. "I can arrange it so that you don't have more than one person. One man only—if it's me. Otherwise there'll be a *lot* of men. They have money and power, these guys, and they can do most anything with you and you wouldn't like it. If you just give yourself to me, and I mean without a fight, I can . . . you know . . . you'd have your own room. There's a boudoir building and you could have your own . . . And I'd make it all easy . . ."

She sat up on the bench and looked at him, surprised at the stab of pity she felt. She could see loneliness, a kind of blurry desperation in his face. But she wasn't going down that road, at all.

"No," she said.

"Gloria . . ."

"Faye. Adullah. And *no*. No one is going to touch me. No one at all, Samuel. Get me out of this prison and then we'll talk about you touching me."

She tried to make it sound believable. But neither of them believed the offer.

"Couldn't do it if I wanted to," he said. He shook his head and looked at her with his eyes narrowed. "Last chance."

"No, Samuel. No. You'll lose an eye, at least, I promise you, if you try it."

He smiled sadly. "Oh no. You'd be out cold. But . . . I don't want it like that."

Gull went to the door, and back into the hall, slammed it shut behind him. His shoes squeaked away, and the sound of the slammed door echoed metallically.

In another cell, someone laughed and someone sobbed, maybe the same person.

• • •

The boudoir was like a cheesy honeymoon motel complete with a red-velvet heart-shaped headboard on the bed. There was a fake window, an illustration of a window on the lavender wall across from the bed, complete with painted-on curtain, and a view of a moonlit landscape. The painting looked pretty amateurish, probably done by an inmate given a special job. The boudoir had a small, red-tiled bathroom, with a shower.

They'd told Faye to take a shower and leave her jumpsuit outside the door of the bathroom, and she had, because she wanted a shower. When she came out, the guards were gone, so was the prison jumpsuit; instead, translucent purple lingerie was laid out on the bed.

"Fuck that," she said. She tossed the lingerie in a corner, and pulled the red satin comforter off the bed. She sat down on the mattress, and worked at the comforter with her teeth, gradually ripping holes in it. By the time the man in the ski mask entered, ushered in by the black badgeless guard, she had a serviceable robe, with her head thrust through a rip in the comforter, other parts of it ripped to make a kind of belt.

"Well that's creative, there, missy," the man said. His voice was gravelly, and very Southwest. Arizona, she judged.

He was a big man wearing a blue and yellow ski mask; a blue silk robe was tied across his bulbous middle; under the robe he wore silky boxers. His legs were pale, short, and slightly bowed. He wore silk slippers. His eyes in the mask holes were small and gray blue.

"Missy? My name is—"

"I don't want to know your name! Mine is Faye Adullah. I'm a reporter. A resident of California. I'm not an inmate. I'm a kidnap victim—"

He raised a hand to stop her. "Everybody has a story. That's yours. They tell me your name is Gloria, so your name is Gloria." He gestured grandly at the bed. "Now Miss Gloria—here's the plan. You lay down over there on that mattress and I'll unwrap the gift that is you. Otherwise I bring the boys in here and they handcuff you. There's some little rings on the side there under the headboard just for that. And you'll be sorry I did that."

"You know, you look like a Mexican wrestler in that mask. Why don't you take it off? Maybe I'll like what I see."

"Not a chance."

"Your voice sounds kind of familiar."

He opened his mouth to speak, thought better of it, then pointed at the bed.

"I guess I need to face facts," Faye said, sighing.

He nodded briskly, once. "That's the spirit."

She sat on the edge of the bed. "Let me see what you've got in those boxers." He sidled nearer. Not quite near enough.

She reached seductively out, stroked his crotch with her right hand. There was an almost immediate response. His eyes went glassy and he stepped closer yet. She stroked downward, pushing the band of the boxers aside, quickly found his testicles, gripped them with all her strength, and twisted. It was an angry grip, and a very hard twist.

"I've been working out," she said, as he squawked, arching his back in pain. "I really think I can rip these right off your body. I've got so much motivation built up! So much juice in me. I think I can do it!"

He writhed and swung hard at her face—she was able to block most of the blow with her left hand. "I'm glad," she said, loud over his yelling, "that you put talcum powder on this dangly ball sack of yours. That way I can keep a grip despite the sweat and—"

He roared with pain and fury and got a jab through, cracking her hard on her left cheekbone. She didn't care. She was a little amused at how unimportant the pain was; how the possibility of real damage didn't matter. She really didn't care. That was kind of funny.

She clawed at his face with her free hand, trying to tear off the mask. He slapped her hand away.

"Goddamnit, *GUARDS!*" he bellowed.

She tightened her grip till she felt her knuckles cracking. He screamed and hit her again. This time he hit her in the right ear, and she heard a reverberating, a gonging, that seemed to announce the warm rush of pain that followed.

She still didn't care. She didn't care if he cracked her head open. She wasn't letting go.

The door opened. Something rolled in. She knew what it was.

Hurt the fucker before the robot stops you.

She tried to tear the man's balls off. He shrieked. She clawed at his face with her other hand. He hit her again. She got a grip on the mask and pulled upward. She saw his red, puffy, sweating face for a moment, and recognized it from her online research. He'd been one of the first to push for Statewide as "the destiny of Arizona."A Congressman . . .

Pursair? That was it. Representative Pursair, from Phoenix.

Then he howled wordlessly at her, trying to dig his thumbs into her eyes.

There was a hissing, a gaseous gushing, a medicinal smell.

Faye was unconscious before she hit the floor.

• • •

Men were talking nearby. She didn't recognize their voices.

"Her organs check out? He smacked her pretty good."

"We're just taking 'em, whatever shape they're in."

"Seems like a waste of a tester."

"The guy was pretty mad. He says no experiments. He says she goes right to organ donation."

"He might need some organs himself. Or anyway glandular donation."

A chuckle. "I think he'll heal up okay."

Faye tried to speak. But her mouth was gummy; her lips rubbery. When she tried to open her eyes it was as if she had to force open steel shutters. She got them open only a crack.

She was lying in an operating room. Two men in white masks, blue caps, blue tops, rubber gloves were on either side of her. One of them had a large syringe in his hand.

It would be fast, anyway. They'd kill her and take the organs. She was okay with it.

A door opened behind them, and they turned, surprised. "Warden . . ."

"New plan," said the stranger. She couldn't see him. A deep-southern voice, maybe Georgia. She'd heard the warden was from Georgia. "Don't touch her. Let her rest in recovery, we're leaving some clothes for her. Get her up to speed."

"Pursair won't like it."

"He'll be okay with it. There's a push to get her out. So . . . Just do it. We've got the bases covered."

She closed her eyes.

Did I imagine all that? Was it a fantasy?

A moment later, the gurney began to roll, whirring on its own power, to some other room . . . away from the operating theater.

She wanted to throw up but she was afraid she'd choke.

Don't throw up.

But she did. They had to turn her over and clear her throat with a tube. She laughed some of the vomit out.

● ● ●

She was waiting for the gate to open. She tightened her fingers on the steering wheel to keep her hands from shaking.

It was midmorning. The sky was overcast; something that wasn't quite heavy enough to be rain drizzled on the windshield. The car sat there idling, its engine barely audible; Faye just sat there too.

She glanced at the gauges. The car had a full charge. She'd be able to drive all the way to Phoenix without stopping.

She looked at her purse again, doing a reality check. The purse beside her was definitely hers. It was sitting on the brown leatherette passenger seat of the McCrue company car.

She repressed the urge to look in her purse again. Everything was there. Faye Adullah's driver's license, her phone, everything. She had already called Phil and left a message. She'd decided not to call anyone else, not yet. No raging calls to the authorities.

Get out first. Don't rock the boat.

Hortense. Her transgender friend had gotten released and taken the message to Phil and Phil must have started calling . . .

The gate was rolling open, left to right. Faye took her foot off the brake, pressed the accelerator. The electric car hummed through the opening almost before it was an opening.

She tried to keep from speeding, as she drove the car up to the access road.

This is real. The sweat on her hands was real. The purse . . . was still there.

"I'm afraid we no longer have your car," Warden Holmes had said. Ervin Holmes was a spruce, well-tanned man who looked almost too young for the job. He had a flat-top haircut, an apologetic sigh in his voice. "We'll be making that good. Your car was crushed at a junkyard, actually. But you can use one of our cars and we'll be in touch about a replacement . . . of course, you'll want to have your lawyer get in touch with us, to work out a settlement . . . We've already arrested a number of . . ."

He'd spoken to her quickly, giving her a cocktail in his office, very apologetic, expecting her to rave at him, seeming relieved when she hadn't.

Faye had found she was barely able to speak to him. She could talk—she was recovered. She was fed and hydrated and dressed in her own clothes and even coddled for a few hours by a female nurse brought in from the outside. She'd asked the Filipino nurse if she knew what was going on here. The nurse had said no, no idea . . .

AzPrisSystem Road 54.

Faye turned right on Road 54. She had directions printed out, on the seat under her purse. She didn't need them. She'd memorized them.

She accelerated to fifty, sixty, seventy miles per hour . . .

There was a thumping, close behind her. And then, a muffled voice.

She slowed down, listening. She heard another thump, with a metallic ring to it. Louder. Then an inarticulate yell filtered by upholstery, metal, fiberglass . . .

Another thump.

Just keep driving.

A harder thump came then, and muffled shouts with an edge of hysteria.

Moaning softly to herself, Faye pulled the car over. She put it in park, touched *Open Trunk*. She heard the trunk pop upward, and a louder shout. A man's voice was clamoring now. A familiar voice.

She opened the door, got out, and walked back to the trunk. Knuckles bloody, Rudy was climbing out clumsily of the trunk, almost falling out.

Automatically, she helped him stand. He had his orange inmate's suit on.

"Rudy . . . ?"

He stood there swaying, mouth slack. "Faye! Where am I? How did I get here?" He reached out, supported himself with one hand on her shoulder. "Are we escaping?"

"Oh no, Rudy. You didn't do this yourself?"

"No. I . . . they drugged me, I think. I can't . . ." He was staring past her, a new alertness coming into his face.

"Faye. Get in the car!"

"What?" She turned to look.

Something reared up, glinting, shuddering, rippling. Its motion didn't seem to fit its size. It was so big. The motion was a little like a whale she'd seen from a boat once. But she knew what it must be.

"The worm," Rudy said, voice haggard. "Faye—get in the fucking car."

"You too, Rudy! Let's go!"

"No way. That thing is fast. They took out your tracker so it's after me. I don't want to fucking live here, Faye." He pushed past her. "And they're not going to let me go."

"Rudy!"

But he was running toward the worm now. Still doped up, he was like a running drunk, wobbling along, almost falling, stumbling sometimes, but picking up speed.

He looked over a shoulder. "Get in the car!" he shouted. "Go!"

The worm was about forty yards back. Rudy was running across the road now, drawing the worm off to the opposite side.

"Fucking *go!*" he shouted, over his shoulder. "Please!"

She turned and walked mechanically to the front of the car—a wave of fear caught up to her, as if it were coming ahead of the worm to get her, to hold her down for it. She had to struggle to make her fingers work on the door handle. She got the car door open, ducked in, stamped the brake, put the car in gear and slammed her foot on the accelerator. The door was still open, a warning chime going off, but she kept accelerating, looking in the mirror just once, to see Rudy facing the worm, his arms upraised in unmitigated terror . . .

The worm slammed down on him like a fly swatter.

She gasped and forced her attention back to driving, and saw she'd wandered over the center line. Another car was rushing toward her. She hit the brakes, twisted the wheel, and her car spun like a carnival ride—then jolted to a stop, the engine dead. Faye sat there hyperventilating, trying to figure out how to get the car going again, her hands trembling.

The car she'd almost hit was backing up. It stopped beside her. "Faye?"

She looked up to see Phil, and two men with him. One of them, in the back seat, was a dark-skinned man wearing a uniform.

For a long moment she thought he was a guard from Statewide and Phil was here to hand her back over to them.

Then she looked closer at the uniform, and saw that it was U.S. Marshals Service.

• • •

"So they weren't letting me go," she said.

Phil shook his head. "It does look like they set you up—'she was helping a prisoner escape.' You were supposed to get killed in the recovery process."

"How many times did I thank you for coming in person?"

"Three. Enough. You want another drink?"

She shook her head. They were sitting in a leather-backed booth, in a dark, fairly noisy bar half a block from the San Diego branch of the Justice Department. It was too early to get drunk, but she thought Phil was close to smashed already. He'd had three vodka gimlets.

She thought about asking him to go to dinner with her, just for the company. But he might misunderstand. He'd feel pressured to come. His wife would be waiting at home . . .

"Anyway," he said, "you should thank Hortense. She wasn't going to leave my damn office till I listened to her. Christ I can't believe you thought I'd set you up!"

"I wasn't exactly thinking rationally then. And no one seemed to check on me."

"They told us you'd blown off the appointment! Said you never showed up at all! We thought you were rescheduling or something. I mean—who thought this shit was going on!"

She almost argued that. But finally, just waved her hand dismissively. "Whatever. I *did* thank Hortense. Took me all day Thursday to find her. We were like hugging and jumping around. She said she'd testify if somebody hid her out somewhere . . ."

"She might have to testify. I'm not sure how seriously she'll be taken in court but . . . you might need her to testify. Statewide's attorneys are still talking as if maybe they're going to go with the story that it was all a mix-up, and your story is some kid of revenge fantasy."

She snorted. "Justice department knows better. The marshals found the girls in there."

He nodded. "You got those women set free, and Skaffel's been arrested, and that Burse woman . . . that's something. I don't know how much more we can get. Almost everyone else is claiming they didn't know anything about Subpod 18 and they say all the organs in the medical annex were from voluntary inmate donors who died of natural causes."

Faye tried to get the young waitress's attention, hoping for a glass of water. The young blond waitress was busy serving sailors from a carrier, laughing with them.

"Phil—Rita Burse, Skaffel, so what? There are hundreds of people there who should be in jail. And what about Pursair?"

"Denials, denials. The Congressman has golfing buddies who says he was with them."

"Yeah I know but—what about getting people in the prison to testify that he was there? What about more arrests? What about investigating *the whole place*? What about a series of stories on Priority Central about the whole damn thing?"

He winced. "Well—you *did* your story."

"It was *cursory*, Phil! They barely let me cover everything and they edited the hell out of it. They *say* they're going to let me do a full story after they do some 'fact-checking' but that just seems like they're blowing smoke. I mean—*are they* going to let me do the story the way I want to?"

Phil licked his lips, and his fingers absently spun his empty glass on the table till it tipped over. He sighed. "Priority Media is going to go with the story that only a few people knew about Subpod 18. And they're not going to follow up on Rudy, or on Pursair . . ."

She stared at him. "When were you going to tell me this?"

"I'm telling you now. I found out while I was waiting for you to come out of the JD interview. I got some calls. I'm sorry but—a number of people on Priority's board of directors have a lot of money in Statewide, Faye. Some of them are pretty major stockholders. And Statewide's so *big . . .*"

"The whole prison system down there needs to be defunded, and just *taken apart*, Phil! Christ, I didn't even scratch the surface! Seven-seventy-five is just one pod out of . . . Phil there are *millions of people in Statewide* from all over the world! It can't be the only place like that! Privatized prisons have almost no oversight—no motivation to stay clean—"

"I know. Maybe other people will look into it. You can always write a book."

"And hope someone publishes it."

"And hope somebody *reads* it," said Phil. "Look, Faye, even if you manage to get the word out, even if you blow the whistle louder and expose the whole thing . . ."

She stared at him. "What? What are you saying?"

"I'm saying, Faye, that nothing really decisive will be done about it. For the simple reason . . ." He shrugged. His eyes looked almost infinitely weary. ". . . that most people aren't like you. Most people just don't seem to care. That's all there is to it. It's just—almost nobody really cares . . ."

NEW TABOOS
AND OTHER UNAUTHORIZED SUGGESTIONS

THE LATE GREAT SCIENCE fiction writer Damon Knight wrote a classic short story called "The Country of the Kind" which tells us about a future society that is civil, humane, poverty-free, and almost without sociopaths. One selfish man is an exception, and is allowed to do as he pleases: stealing, wallowing in other people's homes, anything except for violence; however, he's imprinted with a terrible odor (which he himself cannot sense), and this extremely unpleasant stench warns people when he's coming.

He thinks of himself as the King of the World because he can take what he wants, but in fact he's a pariah.

Recently a headline read, "CEOs Who Collect Billions in Govt Money Demand Cuts to Programs for Poor, Elderly." These same magnates, the "Council of CEOs," seem peeved, very "how dare they" when the American public cries out, at intervals, about the shocking lack of social responsibility big business demonstrates.

But most of the public is not stupid. It's been burned before. It's burned every day. It's been a learning experience.

The public has learned. The contempt corporation PR liaisons have for the public's attention span is palpable; still, people were paying attention when it was revealed in the 1960s and '70s that most major manufacturers were poisoning us with pollution; people were paying attention when it was revealed that those manufacturers dragged their feet, and bit and scratched and struggled, when they were told to curtail their pollution. And people noticed when industry shrieked with wholly unconvincing outrage when it was told to clean up the toxic waste mess it had already made.

People noticed. The billions that the public is forced to spend on clean-ups were noticed. The astounding obliviousness to forethought in the Exxon Valdez and BP Gulf Spill disasters did not go unnoticed.

The public can see that most corporations just don't care unless they're forced to. Despite what may be touted in TV commercials, for every insignificant effort from an oil company on behalf of the environment, there are ten new environmental atrocities somewhere, ten efforts on the part of that industry's lobbyists to squelch laws demanding accountability.

Cancer strikes one in three Americans and kills one in four. According to Samuel Epstein, professor of occupational medicine at the University of Illinois School of Public Health, millions people have died during the last decades in what Epstein calls "this cancer epidemic." Epstein indicates that "there is plenty of evidence that the cancer increase is due to progressive permeation of air, water, food and the workplace with cancer-causing industrial chemicals and pesticides. There is also well-established evidence that a substantial proportion of all cancers is avoidable."

It may be that those deliberately sacrificing lives by knowingly permitting the release of needless carcinogens have convinced themselves that it's all for the sake of a healthy, unimpeded economy. Surely, they tell themselves, people would starve without industry.

In some secret, time-shared corner of their hearts they know full well that we could have industry, and jobs—even more jobs—without polluting, without toxifying, without cheating workers, without underpaying women—if we made the needed investment. Technology doesn't have to pollute. It's like a dog that hasn't been housebroken. To acknowledge that realization, though, would be to curtail their major drive in life: greed, in all its manifestations. The world is their smorgasbord.

Mitt Romney was half right when he said that "corporations are people," since corporate culture is a reflection of its leadership. There are people at the top who give it its character. When they knowingly toxify, when they mistreat workers, when they bust unions and create dangerous working conditions for the sake of higher profits, they think they are "kings of the world"—and so far we have not impregnated them with a bad smell . . .

But we can. Not as literally as in Knight's allegorical story. But we can do it—with New Taboos.

We will still need punitive regulations. But we need something more, something lasting, something impregnated into our beings: the recognition that we aren't alone, that there is no social vacuum.

I suggest that we utilize a social device that is generally either underused or misused. The *taboo*.

Taboos may seem primitive, and indeed many of the old ones are based on archaic religious ideas. But the better taboos are not based on superstition: they are complex, efficient, and self-perpetuating expressions of solid tribal values—that is, of social values.

Before I get to the inevitable list of New Taboos, we have to understand one premise: a thing being forbidden on the surface is not the same as its being truly taboo. A real taboo, worked into the weft and weave of the social fabric, programmed into the very conceptual master-molecule of psychological drives, is much more powerful than simple superficial disapproval.

How do you feel, in your gut, if someone violates a basic taboo and literally craps on your doorstep? Your revulsion, most likely, is profound. That's the profundity of taboo—and it's partly an aesthetic reaction. Violations of taboos are also violations of our aesthetic sense—Damn, that thing is ugly! It may well be that the most refined, evolved taboos are deep aesthetic responses.

We have attached a certain cachet and glamour to "taboo-breaking"—I've basked in that dubious glamour myself. And some taboos are indeed pointless, even socially toxic. The old taboo against talking about sex was surely destructive to healthy psychological development.

But taboos are a tool, and any social tool has its constructive application. Japan has more than its share of taboos, some unhealthy, some healthy. Shoplifting is, happily, so taboo in Japan that security guards in department stores are nearly unknown. In the 1990s, when a Texas college marching-band visited Japan, it was detained before it could return to the States because literally dozens of these sterling American students had shoplifted thousands of dollars' worth of electronic goods from the underguarded Japanese stores. The Japanese were horrified that anyone would do such a thing.

A new slate of taboos could be designated by general proposal and consensus, then imprinted in children through parental drill and kindergarten classes. We would incorporate the new taboos along with such older ones as the taboo against defecating on the sidewalk, public masturbation, peeing on people from rooftops, or more gravely: murder, child molestation, arson, wife-beating, cruelty to animals, and the like. Some of these behaviors still persist despite the taboos—but they are not so prevalent as backward business ethics and greed.

It is unlikely, should we apply this curative, that we'll use the term "taboo" for it, since the term has an atavistic ring. I use it here for clarity. We'll call them something else, but taboos they will be.

A short list of some needed taboos:

It shall be TABOO to toxify the environment. In the short run the severest application of this taboo will be against major polluters; in the long run the other great polluter, the individual who uses household toxins, will also accrue a black mark, less harshly meted.

It shall be TABOO to lie or IN ANY FASHION DE-CEIVE in the process of accumulating money. Business and deception should go together like adult sexuality and children: not at all.

The thought of deceiving people to make money off them should be sickening to us. Currently it's regarded as "marketing skill." It shall be especially taboo to manipulate children into wanting things they don't need, to force them into gender roles . . . or to make small children appear in "pageants" that actually parade parental sexual neurosis.

It shall be TABOO to use political influence for personal gain. It's already disapproved of, even illegal—but to make it taboo is another step. Taboo, remember, goes to the core of our beings, because of the way it's incorporated into society, by doleful repetition and psychological reinforcement, early on.

It shall be TABOO to hide someone else's theft fraud, corporate dishonesty, or criminal pollution, in order to protect one's own part in the system. Only a deeply entrenched psychological revulsion for this sort of thing can eradicate this almost universal tendency.

It shall be TABOO to discriminate on the basis of race or gender or sexual orientation. Self-explanatory.

It shall be TABOO to make an unreasonably large profit—which is arguably a form of theft. But what constitutes "unreasonable?"

I'm talking about thirty-dollar aspirins in hospitals, multi-million-dollar CEO salaries, and undertaxed corporate profits by the major corporations.

The operating of sweatshops and underpaying laborers shall be TABOO. Some formula will be agreed upon, respecting percentage of profits, to decide what degree of low payment is taboo.

It shall be TABOO to permit unnecessary health risks for workers just for the sake of cutting costs. From factories to movie productions.

Torture even for "the greater good" will be TABOO.

It shall be TABOO for national leaders to take a country to war through the use of deception, and it shall be taboo to go to war for any reason other than the most dire necessity.

• • •

Taking Care of Business is one thing; one must be tough and competitive in order to be responsible to oneself and one's family. But lying, cheating, and homicide by negligence (or by sheer cost-cutting callousness) do not constitute Taking Care of Business.

I now seem to hear the voices of people with tattoos of Don't Tread on Me flags; they're reacting to my proposals with weary irritation, or even fury. "Just what we need, another way to impose on us, more people telling us what to do. Or not to do."

But taboos should be used (till we mature past the need), only for those social issues most of us agree on—issues that even the most Libertarian, Don't Tread on Me types would agree on, if they thought it through. Look at my proposals, and you will see that I've only taken basic kindergarten rules of behavior and extended them to the bigger playing fields of commerce and politics: You don't poison the other children. You don't lie, children, and you don't steal. You don't hurt the other kids just to get what you want. You don't take more than your share of the dessert.

On the adult scale, we have laws against some of these social transgressions, but much of the time they're unenforceable. Taboos—if we really integrate them into our society—enforce themselves, for the majority of people. If the taboos are deeply ingrained enough, we don't need the laws.

But how do we punish those, in our hypothetical new system of taboos, who are in violation? If the new taboos are really in place, it will be literally revolting to do business with a polluter. Just to think of it might make you physically ill. Do business with someone who, in the long haul, is responsible for increasing leukemia in children? What a revolting thought! They'll have a social stench about them.

The very concept of pollution will be repugnant. Nowadays we think with horror on the gutters full of feces of medieval Europe. Someday people will think the same way of our own sluicing of pesticides into the rivers and seas, of our toxification of the air, and our radical diminution of forests. How could they have done that? It's . . . sickening! That's the way we should react, as well, to corporate ripoffs, like the defense industry's treasonous willingness to sell bad parts (often imported from China) that risk the lives of young men and women in the armed forces. It should truly, deeply, sicken us. We should react to our marrow.

In order to lend weight to our reactions, we must respond, as a society, to violations of serious ethical and environmental taboos in ways that are clear-cut and strikingly apparent.

Hence, as indicated, taboos for some violations should come equipped with very serious consequences. One is tempted to suggest electric shock, ghastly medications—and was tarring and feathering such a bad idea? But no! We won't stoop to barbarism. The enforcement of New Taboos will begin with economic and social ostracism. Repulsion. Institutions for enforcing New Taboos will be unnecessary. Society's reaction to the stench of such corruption will be the punishment.

Taboos are necessary for now, but they should not be necessary forever. They are a sociological mechanism designed to modify behavior. If we were what we have the potential to be, taboos would be superfluous.

There are those of us who believe that most people are in some degree asleep, even when they suppose themselves to be awake. That is, they go about their day in a kind of trance. According to this theory, far more of our responses are mechanical—purely automatic—than we realize. The exploitation of others is a conditioned reflex; the rationalization of corporate theft or environmental ravage is also conditioned—and partly instinctive. This mechanism is implicitly difficult to escape without the powerful leverages of such tools as taboos and harsh laws.

But there are also those of us who believe that these destructive, psychologically mechanical responses fall away if we recognize our state of walking, waking sleep and strive to awaken from it. If we seek to be more mindful, more conscious, then real consciousness will awaken. And conscience with it.

And then we won't need taboos, old or new.

WHY WE NEED FORTY YEARS OF HELL

1.

IT'S A CONTRADICTION IN terms—two singularities. But there are two: there's the fanciful technological singularity of the imagination, and the singularity that's likely to come about. The false singularity, supposed to come between 2035 and 2045, is almost a "supernatural event" in the minds of many people. With its dream of technologically achieved eternal life, it has the reek of religious mythology about it, the unconscious fear of mortality; the second singularity, the Real Singularity, is more modest but impressive enough . . .

But all technological convergences, revolutions, renaissances, taking place in the next fifty years will happen against the backdrop of social and environmental crises. Multiple simultaneous crises will create shortages, which will further concentrate wealth in the hands of the few, bifurcating the world, separating most of the humanity from the breakthroughs of "singularity" level tech and biotech.

This could result in a powerful and eccentric technocrat class with its own elitist rationale for dominance of the technologically underprivileged through control of media and mechanism. Generally, the moneyed class will be the technologically equipped class; and with some exceptions the disenfranchised financially will be the disenfranchised technologically, despite the cell phones we see now in many remote villages.

Let me be clear that I do not foresee the downfall of civilization. I do not expect my son to have to emulate the Mel Gibson character in *Road Warrior*.

But it's going to be a long slog. Just a few weeks ago the most thorough analysis yet of the world's energy infrastructure, from the International Energy Agency, reported that without significant reduction in greenhouse gases the next *five years* will take us to a point where it will be impossible to hold global warming to relatively safe levels—and the last chance of stopping disastrous climate change will be "lost forever." The door is closing, says their chief economist, in *five years*.

Does anyone think we're going to get global warming under control in *the next five years*? With all the entrenched denialists backed by big oil and the intransigence of companies that profit from burning coal—no! Sadly, it's not going to happen. We *will* feel the full consequences of global warming. When tropical diseases and pests move northward, when monsoons take place in regions unprepared for them, when radical changes in climate impact agriculture, causing dust bowls in some areas and catastrophic flooding in others, we will see a gigantic surge of refugees, hundreds of millions of people, totaling billions globally, moving away from these areas, desperately migrating toward more protected areas.

Oceans provide much of the world's food. Global warming contributes to the acidification of the ocean, which adds to the attrition of fish stocks. Globally, fish supply 60 percent of the protein consumed by the human race, and we have already harmed fish stocks by destructive methods of fishing and pollution.

Food stocks will be radically challenged as climate change increasingly damages agriculture—as it's already doing in Africa. We can anticipate famines that make current food shortages seem like the good old days. And you think western nations are dealing with a lot of refugees now? They are a drop in the bucket.

The social cost of all this will be brutally intimidating. With seven billion people on the Earth, we have about a billion going to bed hungry *right now*, with billions more people coming . . . And it's been observed that the poorest people on earth contribute *least* to climate change but will feel its hand the *heaviest*, since they have the fewest resources with which to adapt and respond.

The massive shifts of large populations will put unprecedented stress on infrastructure and social systems—especially food sources, water, and housing—and will doubtless result in military confrontations. A Pentagon study concluded that under pressure to find new sources of food and safe housing in harsh climate change conditions, some countries will find excuses to invade other countries.

And of course there are other environmental crises arising. It's becoming clearer that fracking to access hydrocarbons does cause earthquakes, and we're doing more and more fracking; this and the reduction in ice pressure on tectonic plates caused by global warming may well cause a great many more earthquakes. And don't forget the *black winds*—toxic fronts of synergized pollutants capable of killing large numbers of people—quite possibly being formed in the upper atmosphere, like an aerial complement to that corresponding giant whirlpool of plastic in the Pacific Ocean. Then there's the delightfully diverse soup of pharmaceuticals (along with other random industrial chemicals) we're finding in aquifers and drinking water. We all know about drugs combining dangerously ("Don't mix those two drugs, dude, bad news!") but we're combining hundreds of them randomly in our water. Sure, they're somewhat diluted, but one wonders when some general, cumulative compound will develop, some drug mix of birth-control pill hormones, steroids, Prozac (one of the most common pollutants in water), antihistamines and antibiotics. What interesting collective neurological side effects might appear? The Romans had their leaded dinner plates . . .

Still, the biggest threat is to food and shelter. And those who have access to resources, feeling threatened, will naturally coalesce defensively against those migrating to seek better conditions. Moneyed, technologically sophisticated elements of society will tend to withdraw from the increasing pressures of the masses of disenfranchised, into the safety of walled, highly protected enclaves, which will be in effect, if not in legal status, technocratic city-states.

2.

A percentage of privileged technocrats may well sink into the repellently self-indulgent decadence of virtual reality retreats, where they'll be sequestered *both* physically and mentally. *Addiction* to social media, videogames, cellphones, and the internet is now a recognized phenomenon and one that has implications for our relationship to future tech. Its addictive capacity will only increase as its experiential quality improves.

It's strange—most of our technology is about extending our reach, but paradoxically, we're in danger of a relationship to technology that actually cuts us off from one another. Cartoonists already caricature families who sit together talking to everyone but each other on their plethora of devices.

There's intelligent collaboration with technology . . . and then there's *mindless dependence* on it. A biomedical engineer has already designed an ECoG (electrocorticography) chip that does not disrupt brain tissue; instead it floats atop the blood-brain barrier, sensing the output of neurons and transmitting them to prosthetic devices, to machinery we wish to control, and so on . . . and some researchers expect the ECoG chip to make electronic telepathy possible.

Nanoengineers at Princeton have developed a superthin electronic skin that puckers and stretches like real skin. It can be adhered invisibly to your forehead; it could be hidden in the throat and used for subvocal communication. It can communicate with the internet, it can transmit data from your body . . . many of you will now be thinking of other examples of human/machine interfacing coming along, and this adds to the *frisson*, the anticipation of a technological "singularity" that supposedly will lead to a kind of *übermensch cyborgian* elite. The fear of death that has generated most of our religious myths has also generated the myth that we can create a second machine body into which we'll supposedly project a copy of ourselves. And—puzzlingly—this recording in a three-dimensional form is regarded as immortality. But the human essence is a whole that's more than the sum of the parts; consciousness still remains mysterious to us, and selfhood is not a series of likes and dislikes recorded into a program.

The real singularity will be simply an unprecedented cybernetic intelligence explosion to many orders of magnitude. That, I do believe, *will* happen—is beginning now, accompanied by a vast increase in interactivity. But the Kurzweilian singularity that allows us to interface with machines until, in his words, "there will be no distinction between human and machine," will not come about sustainably because the psychological and social consequences would be so dire.

People who are quadriplegic have stated that they feel less emotion than they did when they could still feel their entire bodies. The projection of the self into electronics reduces our relationship to the body, the seat of our emotions, and for several reasons that might lead to an increase in psychopathology.

And empathy may be a precious commodity in the future. Most people unconsciously cut off their empathy when they're feeling endangered. When the population increases to eight and nine and ten billion, we may instinctively become, as a race, *less empathetic*—unless we actively struggle against that kind of degeneracy.

The superrich may become *especially* elitist and detached when they get exclusive access to rejuvenation. It's fairly evident that some form of rejuvenation, and certainly extensive life extension, will soon be possible. It is thought that the first person to live three hundred years has recently, somewhere, been born. With a probable ability to grow new replacement organs to suit an individual's DNA in a lab; with Sandia labs' specialized nanoparticles that blast problematic microorganisms and cancers with precise microapplications of drugs; with methods for teasing stem cells into regeneration, regenerative drugs like sirolimus, and other innovations—we will effectively have rejuvenation, for those who can afford it.

Let's be honest. Rejuvenation is sure to be a tremendously expensive process, and it's possible that the *only* the superrich will regenerate. Some of you younger people, now in your twenties, may in seventy-five years be tottering around, quite ancient, and see a youthful Paris Hilton still walking around. Or you may see Dominique Strauss-Kahn, looking younger than he looks right now! Do we want Dominique Strauss-Kahn chasing hotel maids in the year 2095? He'll catch a lot more of them! There are some very good wealthy people in the world, who are showing that they care—I know that—but there is a tendency for many of the superwealthy to be fairly awful, spoiled personalities. We see, hear, and read about them constantly; examples are unavoidable. But we can avoid that fate by making laws that restrict rejuvenation to people who deserve it. You'll get points for art, for science, for good works; add them up and *then* get rejuvenated.

Every technology and every wrinkle of a technology has a dark side. Automated aircraft are supposed to be safer—but the airline industry lately has suffered from what an FAA committee called "automation addiction." Pilots use automated systems for all but a few minutes of the flight—takeoff and landing. They simply program navigation into computers rather than using their hands to fly the plane. And when something goes wrong, they haven't got the skills to deal with it anymore.

Mastery of technology must include acknowledgement of its dark side. Mastery of technology means acceptance of limitations. Limitations have value: for example, limiting the amount of electricity sent through a power line to what that line can safely carry means electrical flow isn't lost.

A machine that pollutes is only partly invented. And a lot of the time we rush into technology so quickly that we don't realize it's going to pollute. It was recently discovered, for example, that every time a garment made from polyester and acrylic fibers is washed, it releases thousands of microplastic fibers that end up fouling coastal environments throughout the globe. No one expected that. No one had thought that form of manufacture through.

Not all biotech innovation will lead to delightful results. People have been enthusiastically breeding dogs of every variety for some time. It's thought that genetic engineering will enable us to create a species of dogs that can talk. Is that a good thing? I love dogs but you may not want your dog to be saying, "Feed me now, I'm hungry, what's in your pocket, what's that smell on your shoes, can we go outside and defecate, and by the way I hate the cat" when you get home from a long day's work.

In a lab in Glasgow, UK, one man is intent on proving that metal-based life is possible. He has managed to build cell-like bubbles from metal molecules and has given them life-like properties. He thinks he will be able to get them to evolve into fully inorganic self-replicating entities. "I am 100 percent positive that we can get evolution to work outside organic biology," claims this researcher. If he's right, we could *breed* the next form of technology.

And it's a little worrisome when you consider that researchers in Seoul, South Korea, and in Bristol, England, have developed plans for something they're calling an *ecobot*—using the Venus Flytrap as a model. The ecobot is a robot that eats. It will be able to ingest flesh and turn it into fuel. Combine the ecobot with the evolving inorganic self-replicating entities planned by the scientist at the University of Glasgow . . . and feel a long slow chill at the thought.

It's time for a philosophy of technology—one that acknowledges its dark side and thinks proactively about the consequences of new technology so that negative consequences can be prepared for. Technology needs to evolve a conscience.

The Real Singularity will offer us some great advances—including a redefinition of what money is, and how it will flow, propelled by a computerized awareness of every significant financial transaction. Paper money will be obsolete and thus money will be thoroughly trackable.

As things stand now, finance is treated like meteorology. Its mysterious ebbs and flows are predicted rather like the way weather is: people forecast recessions and bubbles. The new computing power will make it possible to track almost every movement of monetary units in the world and will bring a complete rethinking of not only economic probability but also the use of money.

Money is purely conceptual, but we act as if it's got a life of its own. We forget that it is a creation of humanity and it can be made to serve humanity as a whole. When that system is enabled there will never have to be another recession. The connectivity that put the Eurozone at risk from the Greek economic meltdown can also protect it—*if* we incorporate complexity theory and computer modeling. Or so we're told by Len Fisher, a physicist at the University of Bristol. "Cascades of failure may be controlled by changing the nature and strength of the links between various parts of the networks," says Fisher. I envision a computer that would have access to a pool of funds that it would use to prevent crises.

But yes—there will be catastrophe between here and there. I believe that catastrophe will spur social transformation. We'll have astounding technological advancement against a backdrop of grievous social inequity and quite possibly increasing barbarity, *for a period*, until we are forced by waves of crises to come to terms with the consequences of developing a civilization blindly. Wars, plagues, radical separation of privileges, famines due to climate change and other environmental consequences, will force humanity to accept Buckminster Fuller's "Spaceship Earth" concept as very real.

In short, we will be forced by the dire situation we find ourselves in, to stop whining about world government. Only world government—one committed to human rights (including the rights of women, which are integral to population control) and environmental justice—can deal with these kinds of international crises. World government will not mean anyone gives up their culture, except the bits that reject human rights; it will not be a great gray conformity; there will still be at least as much national sovereignty, for most issues, as states in Europe have in the EU. And remember that the EU, a fuzzy foreshadowing of world government, is in a very early stage. It's having problems, and that was inevitable—it's still evolving! But it does have the right idea. Toward the end of the twenty-first century the world will move toward a framework of consensus on some basic rules regarding population growth, the environment, and access to technology. Empowering Third World people with education and technology will give them a step toward the resources and coping ability they'll need to survive.

I believe we'll achieve a collective progressive consciousness as a result of the revelatory shocks we'll endure in the next fifty years. We'll learn we can't treat Spaceship Earth as a party cruise ship.

Thank you. Any questions?

"PRO IS FOR PROFESSIONAL"
JOHN SHIRLEY INTERVIEWED BY TERRY BISSON

You're tough to pigeonhole, John. You are celebrated as a post-modernist in McCaffrey's Storming the Reality Studio, *but you are generally published as a genre writer. Is there a contradiction? Or is this a postmodernist disguise?*

I never felt like a postmodernist in the philosophical sense, but I can appreciate its forward-looking sensibility and its relativism. I believe in having a moral and ethical compass, but I'm down on dogmatism.

I'm a genre writer partly because I make my *living* as a writer, and that's where the market was for a guy like me when I started. Also, science fiction seemed to me to be in line with the surrealism I admired in art. The genre has its appeal—it provides a kind of literary computer program, where you can model alternative societies and various social futures, and see what might work and what might break down, and what the unintended consequences of trends might be. And it seemed to be a place for outsiders to find a role—and it was. Look, they even took Terry Bisson in! And, for example, Alice Sheldon . . .

William Gibson felt like an outsider too. He once said in an interview (paraphrasing here) that if a weird cat like Shirley can find a niche there, so can I. So some genres are places for outsiders to find a home. And where else can you get paid to create bizarre imagery?

But I'm an outsider within genre writing too. I am. And of course I like to pretend to transcend genre, to be *sui generis* . . .

How did you get started as a writer? Was there a breakthrough moment or book that made it real?

I published in the alternative press at first, around 1970, so that helped. But really it was the Clarion writer's workshop. I was accepted to that and had a small windfall that made it possible to pay for it. I was bottled up at Clarion with the likes of Ursula Le Guin, Harlan Ellison, Frank Herbert, Avram Davidson, Terry Carr, Robert Silverberg. I was there with Gus Hasford, who went on to write *The Short-Timers* [the novel that was the basis for the film *Full Metal Jacket*], and Vonda McIntyre, Lisa Tuttle, Art Cover—a group of talent-charged people.

I was barely civilized at the time. Ellison jeered at the reek of my dorm room. I took acid there one day. But still—I got a great deal out of the basic Clarion experience. Especially criticism—the criticism I received was golden.

My first pro publication was in a Clarion anthology. Carr and Silverberg went on to accept stories by me for their anthologies. Damon Knight's Milford West workshops in

Eugene were a great help. He and Kate Wilhelm taught us—Joe Haldeman and Gene Wolfe were students, with me, back then! They taught me to read my own writing as a reader would and that helped mature my prose, which was necessary because it was often, well, *premature*, as it were.

I think of cyberpunk as SF plus noir (or vice versa). How would you describe it? After all, you were there.

Your description is not far from mine. And I always quote Gibson: "The street has its own uses for things." People on the street, or the poor, the underclasses, can appropriate technology and use it against the power structure; use it to challenge the status quo. Look what happened in the Arab Spring. Look what Anonymous does, or WikiLeaks. It's not all good. But it's all cyberpunk.

"Dystopian" seems a rather gentle euphemism for the worlds you create. Have you ever written a utopian novel or story?

I sometimes take things in a metaphysical direction—I prefer that term to "spiritual." I'm influenced by Aldous Huxley, who did that so well in *Time Must Have a Stop*, and *The Perennial Philosophy*. In those metaphysical explorations we find doorways "out" of the worst of the human dilemma; or a transcendence of it—a right relationship to our condition. Right congruence.

Usually even my darkest novels, like *Everything Is Broken* or *Demons*, have a resolution where things are at least improved; where there's hope, a direction to go in. But getting there can be hell.

The Other End is a novel of alternative apocalypse, where I make up the Judgment Day I'd like to see. It's a Judgment Day without an angry God, but there's still . . . something. And that's a kind of utopian vision, I guess.

The idea of city personified animates your classic City Come A-Walkin'. *Fritz Leiber had a different take on the same theme (and same city) in* Our Lady of Darkness. *Was the old German an influence?*

I don't think I read *Our Lady of Darkness*, but another Germanic fellow (he was Swiss) was an influence: Carl Jung. *City Come A-Walkin'* is a bit influenced by Jung's ideas of the collective unconscious, but mostly influenced by my stays in San Francisco at an impressionable time, and by the music and lyrical content of Patti Smith. I simply perceived cities that way—each had its own mind. City as a kind of organism. *City Come A-Walkin'* was also influenced by my involvement in progressive, edgy, pre-punk rock 'n' roll. I was trying to capture that feel, that energy, that pulse.

I have always tried to fuse things, to bring contrasting art forms into some kind of creative unity. It seems contradictory to fuse storytelling with surrealism (hence someone had to make up the term "magic realism")—real surrealism shouldn't be rational enough to have the internal logic of a story. But I have tried, anyway, and succeeded at times, or so I am told. J.G. Ballard of course did it in novels like *The Crystal World*. He has always been an inspiration.

I often think of SF and Fantasy as this jumble shop of ideas to be examined, reused, appropriated, and returned—a commons, if you will. Your thoughts on the copyright/commons debate. Should music be free? What about literature?

I'm a person who makes a living from intellectual property. I have an album—mostly songs, not readings—that came out in January 2013, from Black October Records. So I don't leap headlong into Creative Commons for books and music.

Having said that, I do think it's possible to worry too much about, say, free music downloading. *South Park* made fun of Metallica: the poor Metallica musician had to buy a *slightly smaller* private jet because of music piracy! Well, I don't have a private jet but I don't like it when *The Crow* (I was co-scripter for the movie) is pirated, as I get money from DVD sales.

And yet my son has almost convinced me that there's room for it all. For example, a lot of artists put free stuff up on YouTube to publicize their work. If you offer a song free, people will buy your album. I have some of my short stories free at my blog in hopes of encouraging people to buy books.

Tell us about your work with Blue Öyster Cult. Was this a natural fit?

I wrote lyrics for them—eighteen songs. BOC is "the thinking man's hard rock band." Their music is intricate, their lyrics vary between deliberately ironic and chilling. They often used horror and science fiction imagery, stuff that had the resonance of Lovecraft or Bradbury. They had a vision of a dark underlying reality behind the accepted human world, and I identified with that point of view. You find something like that in the shadowy organizations behind a futuristic neofascism in *A Song Called Youth*, my cyberpunk trilogy—even though I tend to disdain conspiracy theories.

And in fact my first novel is called *Transmaniacon*, which is the name of a Blue Öyster Cult song. In my rather jejune way I dedicated it to them and to Patti Smith (who also wrote lyrics for the Blue Öyster Cult—as did Michael Moorcock). The band was aware of me because of the book, and many years later I got the invitation to write lyrics for them. And jumped at it.

The Crow has a dark history. What was your share in all that?

I found the comic, which was obscure, took it to a producer who optioned it (attaching me as screenwriter). It's not an accident the comic was movie-like, since James O'Barr, the creator of *The Crow*, was into Japanese samurai films. I wrote the first four drafts of the script but didn't get along with one of the producers.

I wanted to have a ruthless corporate scumbag be the main bad guy in *The Crow*, but the producer I had the run-in with came from a family that owned a big corporation. He insisted on changing it, I argued with him, and soon I was out. They brought David Schow in for a rewrite, and he did fine. So Schow and I share the credit.

Obviously the real shadow on *The Crow* was the death of its star, Brandon Lee, during filming. Just an accident, something stuck in the barrel of a prop gun, and a powerful blank shell . . . but it could have been avoided. The movie was mostly done when he died, and they paid a settlement, then finished the film in post, and it was a hit. All in all it was a good movie, seething with stylistic originality, because despite the tragic accident, it had the right director, Alex Proyas.

Any movie projects in the works? There were rumors about Demons . . .

My novel *Demons* has been optioned a few times. The Weinstein brothers optioned and reoptioned it, and they had a director attached, and a script. But then the recession hit, and the Weinsteins almost went broke. They had to ditch most of their film projects and refinance, so the film was dropped.

But there's interest, still. *Demons* is a nightmarish novel, with spiritual overtones, having to do with demons invading Earth the way hostile extraterrestrials do in other tales. And it's an allegory about how far industry is willing to go in sacrificing innocent people for the sake of profits . . .

Your nonfiction book on Gurdjieff shows not only an understanding but a sort of affinity. How did this project come about?

It was the product of fifteen some-odd years of intense reading in spirituality and philosophy. People like Alan Watts and Aldous Huxley and William James and Meister Eckhart and Lao Tzu and Ramakrishna and Emerson and Thoreau. Zen writers like Shunryu Suzuki. Sufism, Christian mysticism, certain forms of Gnosticism—even old C.S. Lewis. In philosophy, Plato (the *Timaeus* dialogue), Spinoza . . .

Then I read an interview with Jacob Needleman about Gurdjieff's ideas on the human condition. And I felt, yeah, that's right! Needleman's book *Time and the Soul* had a great influence on my thinking. So I became a student of Needleman and, through him, of Gurdjieff. Essentially, Gurdjieff says that we're all psychological machines; that we're asleep when we think we're awake. But even though we are unconscious, there are moments of freedom and liberation. And it's possible to develop something inwardly that can be freer yet, and more conscious.

Me, I wanted practical results. I didn't want to jabber about spirituality. I wanted to be free. I wanted to be in command of myself—I'd been such a bull in a china shop, in my life! Most of all I wanted to be more conscious. How could I get there, practically speaking? The Gurdjieff Foundation provided specific methods. To my astonishment, the methods really helped. I am not conscious, but I can see the signposts to a fuller consciousness.

So when Penguin gave me the chance to do a serious book on the subject, an intro to Gurdjieff's life and ideas, I jumped at it.

But while I'm influenced by Gurdjieff, and use his methods, I'm influenced by Zazen methodology too, and by the teachings of Krishnamurti. Yet it's not a vague mishmash. I am focused on a specific methodology, one you find in all the greatest metaphysical traditions, when you get to their inner, esoteric circle.

You have strong connections in cyberpunk, in underground comics, and in rock music. How did this come about? Does it all still fit together?

It overlaps more than fits together. Frank Zappa influenced underground comics; underground comics—for example, the work of Paul Mavrides and Jay Kinney and [Victor] Moscoso and Spain Rodriguez—influenced me, and so did Zappa and so did Captain Beefheart and so did King Crimson . . . and so did composers like Stravinsky and Varèse, for that matter. And Penderecki.

Groups as diverse as Blue Öyster Cult, the Rolling Stones, the Sisters of Mercy, Hawkwind, the Velvet Underground, artists like Jimi Hendrix, Patti Smith, Iggy Pop, John Lydon . . . they were all voracious readers. Most of them had read the better science fiction. Patti Smith was especially influenced by Baudelaire and Verlaine, as I was. And people in that scene had an appreciation for filmmakers like Fellini, like Kubrick, like Roeg . . .

Somehow it all made up a counterculture to the counterculture. We were outside the counterculture per se; we were our own underground counterculture, and it all overlapped.

Which do you like better, writing for TV or for comics (leaving aside the money)?

I've only written for comics once: a five-issue mini series for IDW: *The Crow: Death and Rebirth*, which is a sort of reboot of *The Crow* set in Japan (and in Japanese Buddhist hell). It was a good experience in some ways, frustrating in others, but I got my story told. It's out in a graphic novel now.

So I haven't had that much experience with comics. But it wasn't as committee-oriented, in terms of the writing, as television. You're always filtered through producers and executives, "suits," in TV and movies. Few people get to be *auteurs*. I'm still waiting for my first really satisfying film or TV writing experience. I had a bit more artistic freedom writing the comic.

Do you have a daily routine as writer? A certain bow tie, an heirloom chair, a time or word-count quota? (People like to know these things.)

So you know about the bow tie and the chair? Well, it's true: I tie a bow on a chair, and then the chair tells me what to write.

Beyond that, I try not to get up too late in the day, I try not to spend too much time online, and I usually end up writing from about noon till three. I take a break, then write till dinner. If I'm writing a work-for-hire piece I assign myself a certain number of pages per day. If I'm writing out of my own wellspring of inspiration, which naturally I prefer, I try to write at least five pages. Sometimes it will be more. Thank God for revision. I often start the writing day by revising what I wrote the previous day to get into the swing of the narrative.

That's fiction. Nonfiction, of course, I write nude, on my roof (in all weathers), wearing a balloon-animal hat.

What are you reading right now for fun?

Are we allowed to read for fun? I usually read biographies or historical fiction, at this time in my life. Now reading *1356* by Bernard Cornwell. I'm also a big fan of Patrick O'Brian and tend to reread him. I like reading something that edifies me and entertains me at the same time. Guilt free!

Did you learn anything useful from your stint in the Coast Guard?

Sure. I learned that I had a hell of a lot to learn. I learned that I was a clumsy, fairly absurd, loutish young snot. I learned respect for men who risk their lives to rescue people, too. It was all a bit like Kipling's *Captains Courageous*, but I didn't pull it off as well as his snotty boy did.

There is a persistent theme in your work: the battle between the young and the old. The good guys being usually the young. Has this changed over the years?

Not entirely. Over the years, I've accrued more understanding of elders, and of some traditions. But of course lots of traditions are vile and need to be dumped. Racism is traditional, customary in some places—a thing being customary doesn't make it good.

You will of course find more older people in my novels now that I've grown up. But when reediting earlier books I find I still connect with most of the writing. My *A Song Called Youth* (I think of it as one novel, and it is—in the Prime Books omnibus) was titled that because I knew, even back then, that youth has its own point of view. And it's all relative.

A reader described Everything Is Broken, *your anti-libertarian thriller, as* Atlas Shrugged *turned on its head (a contortionist metaphor worthy of Cirque du Soleil!). What inspired that work?*

Ugh, I hate to be compared to Ayn Rand at all. If it's on its head, it's because my thinking is the opposite of Ayn Rand's. What inspired the book was a reaction against Randian thinking, against Libertarianism, against the Tea Party. *Everything Is Broken* is a crime novel/disaster novel fusion that, underlyingly, is also an allegory about the value of community and the need to fight back against the Ayn Rands out there.

How would you describe your politics?

While I can see some virtue in some selfishness, and I believe in independent thinking and constantly critiquing government, I think we still have a profound need for a well-organized, democratic, centralized government. I have a streak of socialist in me, but I believe in a free market modified by regulation; capitalism modified by, for example, socialized medicine, social safety nets. It's not a choice between government and anarchy. It's about allowing some space for the anarchic in a structured society.

I'd like to see Elizabeth Warren run for president. We need a woman president next time. Hopefully, if it's not Warren, our woman president will be a progressive Independent, or a Democrat.

What was your intro to Left politics?

I think seeing the photos of the My Lai massacre, when I was a boy, influenced me to ask: What the *hell* is going on? Those grim, grisly color photos of murdered women and children radicalized me. Years later my radicalization was moderated by experiences on the street, back when I was a drug user. I came to appreciate a properly run police force.

Looking at history, I see some social progress—like the end of legal slavery and the beginning of empowering women. The rise of unions helped establish the middle class. Some of that's been undone, but the fight goes on. I appreciate the Occupy movement. It didn't have a clear message but no one else was doing anything that honest. Some of those people will in time develop a more effective political movement, and I'll welcome it.

What do you find most frustrating about the Left? Is the Right right about anything?

I find kneejerk political correctness frustrating; I find the Left's self-righteousness and lack of pragmatism frustrating. And the sheer cynicism of many who *were* on the Left and now just shrug and sneer—that, too, I find frustrating.

I think we need conservatives. It's a kind of thesis, antithesis, synthesis thing, and we need them to push back against us, within reason. But you know, even conservatives get "progressive" after a while. Few of them would consider taking the vote from women. They digested that much social evolution. They have digested some degree of environmentalism—and now in the age of global warming they're getting a real schooling.

And conservatives are correct that unions can be exploitative, and too expensive for a community if they become greedy. Only, that shouldn't mean getting *rid* of unions—it should mean *modifying* unions, a bit. It doesn't justify the kind of union-busting on a state level we're seeing now, in places like Michigan.

What do you mean by "reverse terraforming"?

Turning the habitable world into an uninhabitable world through world war or environmental irresponsibility. Like global warming.

Do you think writers have a particular social responsibility? What is it, then?

I only know that I personally have a sense of social responsibility—yet as a writer I also feel another kind of responsibility: to entertain. It's a balance. Dickens was powerfully entertaining—but he sure made his point, and a sharp, penetrating point it was. There were actual social reforms prodded into being by his novels. Steinbeck, Upton Sinclair—more than once, novelists have prompted reforms.

Yes, I know, we've gotten stuck with Fox News now, and the *Citizens United* decision, the Koch brothers. We're in danger of falling into a corporatist dictatorship. But we're not there yet, and books like *Brave New World* and *1984* and *Fahrenheit 451* have helped. So did books like *Catch-22*. Solzhenitsyn schooled us about the excesses of USSR-style communism. *Uncle Tom's Cabin* helped end slavery. Novels can be our social conscience.

Have you ever collaborated with anybody besides E.A. Poe? How did it work out?

The Poe collaboration was just finishing an unfinished story by him, in an anthology called *Poe's Lighthouse*. I hope he approves of my collaborative efforts but I haven't heard from him. Yet.

I've also collaborated on stories with Rudy Rucker, William Gibson, Marc Laidlaw, and Bruce Sterling. That's good shit, man.

Ever been attacked by wild monkeys?

Oh, you laugh. We'll likely all be attacked by them, and other tropical creatures, as global warming chases them north! The worst will be the diseases, though. Say hello to tsetse flies, Montana.

You wrote of drones (in A Song Called Youth*, if I remember correctly) long before they flew into the consciousness of the public. Do you ever worry that the CIA is mining your books for ideas?*

I was recently told by someone that he gave the early version of those novels (I've since revised and updated them) to people high in the U.S. military in the early '90s. However, I refuse to apologize to al-Qaeda.

The military has confessed to mining ideas from *Star Trek* and Arthur Clarke and Larry Niven. In *A Song Called Youth* the drones are basically a tool of the oppressors. The heroes of the novels are the resistance to a corporatist neofascist theocracy—and drones represent danger. And some of that's coming true.

But I think drones can be used legitimately. Sometimes. Better get used to them. Police forces are buying them up.

What kind of car do you drive? (I ask this of everyone.)

A Toyota Echo on its last legs, if it had legs. I want to get a Chevy Volt next.

There's a legend that you introduced William Gibson to SF. True?

The legend has it backward. I introduced science fiction to Gibson. He was already a reader of SF (and a great deal more). He had already published one piece in an obscure SF zine called *UnEarth*. I showed his unpublished stories to the editors of *OMNI*, and to Terry Carr. Carr later bought his novel *Neuromancer*.

But what really "introduced" Gibson was his excellence as a writer. When I read his stories I was immediately impressed by his wit and the beginning of what was to be a kind of literary mastery. It was like hearing Eric Clapton play guitar for the first time. "Yeah, man, he can play."

Do you prefer writing short stories or novels? Does one ever morph into the other?

I have shamelessly woven short stories into novels for years and have developed novellas, like *Demons*, into novels. You bet. I'm a pro, that's one thing pros do. No, "pro" there is not short for prostitute, it's short for professional.

R.A. Lafferty? Ayn Rand? Rudy Rucker? Hunter Thompson? Each in one sentence please.

Lafferty had an incomparable originality in his way of looking at the world, which showed me that good science fiction didn't have to be science-based. Ayn Rand ended her life on welfare. Rudy Rucker is a lead guitarist of ideas. Hunter Thompson was a huge talent who perhaps influences some writers too much.

Do you listen to music when you write?

I typically do, as it seems to soak up distractions, for me at least, and it creates atmosphere and even conveys energy—but it has to be music of a certain order. The lyrics can't be out in front or on top; I can't be listening to Dylan while writing or I'll start writing Dylanesquely. Instrumental music works if it has the right feel—if it feels like the "soundtrack" of what I'm writing. I can also listen to certain bands where the lyrics don't intrude. Mostly they don't intrude because they're embedded in a wall of sound. Like Motörhead, for example, or the Stooges' *Funhouse* album. Rammstein is ideal because it's high energy, the right mood, and the lyrics aren't distracting because they're mostly in German so they're just sounds to me.

What city is best for writers today? Tomorrow? If it were 2056, what city would you want to live in?

New York City is always best for novelists. That's where most of the publishers are, hello. I lived there for years and loved New York. I'd live there again in a hot second. I live in the next best place now—the San Francisco area, which is pretty agreeable to writers and artists. Lots of smart, stimulating people here. Stories on every corner.

If you're writing films, well, you don't *have* to be in LA but it can help. So it's about the people you interface with. However, for some people the best place to write might be deep in a redwood forest.

In 2056 I want to be under the dome that's protecting Seattle, maybe, or Toronto. Cooler, safer. The Black Winds will be blocked off by the dome. Defensible . . .

When they do the John Shirley biopic, who do you want to play yourself? (And don't say Johnny Depp; he doesn't have your looks.)

William Hurt could play me as I am now. Me as a young person, I don't know—some actor yet to be discovered who can play "out-of-control youth" and embody paradox. Good and bad, kind and selfish, hardworking and slothful. As a youth I was all those things at once.

I know you and your wife Micky take film seriously. What filmmakers do you watch? What bands or musicians? What writers?

These days I'm pretty eclectic about film. I like Peter Jackson's stuff and I enjoyed the *John Carter* movie and *Skyfall*. But I also like, say, Terrence Malick, and David

Fincher. I like certain Korean filmmakers, Bong Joon-ho or Park Chan-wook. I like the Swedish filmmaker Tomas Alfredson. I think some really creative stuff is being done in science fiction films these days, like *Chronicle* and *Looper.*

Did cyberpunk die . . . or do a butterfly?

It was eaten alive, co-opted. Today it shows up in film and television, it's in comics, it's even in some so-called "military" SF. But that's justice. We cyberpunks devoured and digested Philip Dick, Alfred Bester, Cordwainer Smith, Ellison, Delany, John Brunner . . .

My Jeopardy item: The answer is, Fox News. You provide the question.

What news channel should someone with a conscience and deep pockets buy? Please!

You seem to keep a line open to Hollywood. Ever tempted to live in LA?

I have lived in Los Angeles and would again if I had the right project there, something I needed to be on site for. I'd love to be hands-on, a producer on a show of my creation, so I could choose what really matter: the writers, the directors, the actors. In that order of importance.

If you are ever elected U.S. president, what will be your first executive order?

Not sure, probably something environmental. I will pick the one that will most annoy the Tea Party types.

BIBLIOGRAPHY

Novels:

Transmaniacon (New York: Zebra, 1979)

Dracula in Love (New York: Zebra, 1979; 1990)

City Come A-Walkin' (New York: Dell, 1980; Asheville, NC: Eyeball Press, 1996; New York: Four Walls Eight Windows, 2001)

Three-Ring Psychus (New York: Zebra, 1980)

The Brigade (New York: Avon, 1981)

Cellars (New York: Avon, 1982; Akron, OH: Infrapress, 2006)

Eclipse (*A Song Called Youth* Trilogy book one) (New York: Warner Books/Popular Library, 1985; Northridge, CA: Babbage Books, 2000)

In Darkness Waiting (New York: Onyx/New American Library, 1988; Akron, OH: Infrapress, 2005)

Kamus of Kadizar: The Black Hole of Carcosa (New York: St. Martin's Press, 1988)

Eclipse Penumbra (*A Song Called Youth* Trilogy book two) (New York: Warner Books/Popular Library, 1988; Northridge, CA: Babbage Books, 2000)

A Splendid Chaos (New York: Franklin Watts, 1988; Northridge, CA: Babbage Books, 2006)

Eclipse Corona (*A Song Called Youth* Trilogy book three) (New York: Questar/Popular Library, 1990; Northridge, CA: Babbage Books, 2001)

Wetbones (Shingletown, CA: Mark V. Ziesing, 1991; New York: Leisure, 1999)

Silicon Embrace (Shingletown, CA: Mark V. Ziesing, 1996)

Demons (Baltimore: Cemetery Dance Publications, 2000; New York: Ballantine Books, 2002)

The View from Hell (Burton, MI: Subterranean Press, 2001)

Her Hunger, short novel in *Night Visions 10*, edited by Richard Chizmar (Burton, MI: Subterranean Press, 2001).

. . . And the Angel with Television Eyes (San Francisco: Night Shade, 2001)

Spider Moon (Baltimore: Cemetery Dance Publications, 2002)

Demons, new version with second novella *Undercurrents* (New York, Del Rey, 2002)

Crawlers (New York: Del Rey, 2003)

Subterranean, Constantine Hellblazer tie-in (New York: Pocket Star, 2006)

The Other End (Baltimore: Cemetery Dance Publications, 2007)

Black Glass (Chicago: Elder Signs Press, 2008)

Bleak History (New York: Pocket Books, 2009)

BioShock: Rapture, gaming tie-in novel (New York: Tor, 2011)

Everything Is Broken (Rockville, MD: Prime Books, 2012)

A Song Called Youth, complete trilogy, omnibus plus individual e-books of *Eclipse*, *Eclipse Penumbra*, and *Eclipse Corona* (Gaithersburg, MD: Prime Books, 2012)

Nonfiction:

Gurdjieff: An Introduction to His Life and Ideas (New York: Tarcher, 2004)

Collections:

Heatseeker (Los Angeles: Scream, 1989)

New Noir (Boulder, CO: FC2/Black Ice, 1993)

The Exploded Heart (Asheville, NC: Eyeball, 1996)

Black Butterflies (Shingletown, CA: Mark V. Ziesing, 1998; New York: Leisure, 2001)

Really Really Really Really Weird Stories (San Francisco: Night Shade Books, 1999)

Darkness Divided (Lancaster, PA: Stealth Press, March 2001)

Living Shadows: Stories: New and Pre-Owned (Rockville, MD: Prime Books, 2007)

In Extremis: The Most Extreme Stories of John Shirley (Portland: Underland Press, 2011)

Selected Screenplays:

The Crow - first writer, shares screenplay credit

The Specialist - movie was based on novel written under a
 pseudonym

Primal Scream/Twists of Terror - TV movie for the
 Showtime Channel

Mysterium - TV movie for Fox Channel based on the
 novel by Robert Charles Wilson

Hunter Prime - based on novels by Robert Sheckley (sold
 to Pressman/Jeff Most productions)

ABOUT THE AUTHOR

JOHN SHIRLEY IS AN author, screenwriter, and songwriter. The author of more than thirty science fiction, horror, urban fantasy, and dark crime novels, he has garnered praise from many directions including the *New York Times Book Review*, Clive Barker, Peter Straub, William Gibson, the *Washington Post*, and *Publishers Weekly*.

He won the Bram Stoker Award for his story collection *Black Butterflies*. He was co-screenwriter of *The Crow* and has written for television shows such as *Deep Space Nine*. He has written one nonfiction book, *Gurdjieff: An Introduction to His Life and Ideas* (Penguin Tarcher). His cyberpunk trilogy, *A Song Called Youth*, is known for its sharp geopolitical predictions and progressive point of view. His newest novel *Everything Is Broken*, is a near-future crime novel showing how "Tea Party" thinking could lead to social disaster.

Shirley has cowritten eighteen songs for the Blue Öyster Cult and his own bands. Black October Records has recently brought out a double CD, *Broken Mirror Glass*, a selection of his recordings from 1978 to 2012.

He lives in the San Francisco Bay Area with his wife.

PM PRESS
OUTSPOKEN AUTHORS

Report from Planet Midnight
Nalo Hopkinson
128 Pages
$12.00

Nalo Hopkinson has been busily (and wonderfully) "subverting the genre" since her first novel, *Brown Girl in the Ring*, won a Locus Award for SF and Fantasy in 1999. Since then she has acquired a prestigious World Fantasy Award, a legion of adventurous and aware fans, a reputation for intellect seasoned with humor, and a place of honor in the short list of SF writers who are tearing down the walls of category and transporting readers to previously unimagined planets and realms.

Never one to hold her tongue, Hopkinson takes on sexism and racism in publishing ("Report from Planet Midnight") in a historic and controversial presentation to her colleagues and fans.

Plus...

"Message in a Bottle," a radical new twist on the time travel tale that demolishes the sentimental myth of childhood innocence; and "Shift," a tempestuous erotic adventure in which Caliban gets the girl. Or does he?

And Featuring: our Outspoken Interview, an intimate one-on-one that delivers a wealth of insight, outrage, irreverence, and top-secret Caribbean spells.

PM PRESS OUTSPOKEN AUTHORS

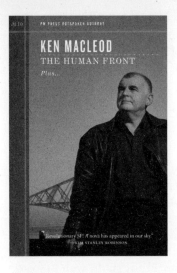

The Human Front
Ken MacLeod
128 Pages
$12.00

Winner of a Prometheus and Sidewise Award, and largely unavailable this side of The Pond, *The Human Front* follows the adventures of a young Scottish guerrilla, drawn into low-intensity sectarian war in a high-intensity future, when the arrival of an alien intruder (complete with saucer) calls for new tactics and strange alliances.

MacLeod's unique vision is developed even further in a new commentary written especially for this edition, and in his delightful personal account of a Hebridean youth's first encounter with the post-capitalist world. Also featured is our Outspoken Interview showcasing the author's deep erudition and skeptical, mordant wit.

> "*The Human Front* has pretty much everything you could ask from a great story: character, insight, plot, that quality of description that transports a feeling, sensation, incident or landscape seemingly direct from world to mind, and revelation. It has substance. It should make your mind reel, and work."
> —Iain M. Banks

> "*The Human Front* is a feather-weight book, which packs a heavyweight punch. In terms of size, it's a novella, but it includes more entertainment than many books that are four times its length."
> —Nathan Brazil, SF Site

"Dazzling! Fowler is one of a kind."
—MINNEAPOLIS STAR TRIBUNE

PM PRESS
OUTSPOKEN AUTHORS

The Science of Herself
Karen Joy Fowler
128 Pages
$12.00

Well known in the mainstream for her bestseller, *The Jane Austen Book Club*, Karen Joy Fowler offers a short collection of perceptive, entertaining, thought-provoking, and often hilarious speculative stories with a progressive and feminist edge.

An all-new story set in the days of Darwin, "The Science of Herself" is an astonishing hybrid of SF and historical fiction: the almost-true story of England's first female paleontologist and her struggles to bring modern science to the Victorian establishment. "The Further Adventures of the Invisible Man" is a hilarious faux-YA tale about bullying, revenge, baseball, and shoplifting. "The Motherhood Statement," a nonfiction analysis of the current state of gender equality in publishing and politics, shows off Fowler's radicalism and impatience with conservative homilies and liberal pieties alike.

Also featured is our Outspoken Interview, in which the author tells us what kind of car she drives, what she watches on TV, and what it's like to hit the *Times* bestseller list.

> "No contemporary writer creates characters more appealing, or examines them with greater acuity and forgiveness, than she does."
> —Michael Chabon, author of *The Amazing Adventures of Kavalier & Clay*

FRIENDS OF

These are indisputably momentous times—the financial system is melting down globally and the Empire is stumbling. Now more than ever there is a vital need for radical ideas.

In the six years since its founding—and on a mere shoestring—PM Press has risen to the formidable challenge of publishing and distributing knowledge and entertainment for the struggles ahead. With over 250 releases to date, we have published an impressive and stimulating array of literature, art, music, politics, and culture. Using every available medium, we've succeeded in connecting those hungry for ideas and information to those putting them into practice.

Friends of PM allows you to directly help impact, amplify, and revitalize the discourse and actions of radical writers, filmmakers, and artists. It provides us with a stable foundation from which we can build upon our early successes and provides a much-needed subsidy for the materials that can't necessarily pay their own way. You can help make that happen—and receive every new title automatically delivered to your door once a month—by joining as a Friend of PM Press. And, we'll throw in a free T-shirt when you sign up.

Here are your options:
- $25 a month: Get all books and pamphlets plus 50% discount on all webstore purchases
- $40 a month: Get all PM Press releases (including CDs and DVDs) plus 50% discount on all webstore purchases
- $100 a month: Superstar—Everything plus PM merchandise, free downloads, and 50% discount on all webstore purchases

For those who can't afford $25 or more a month, we're introducing Sustainer Rates at $15, $10, and $5. Sustainers get a free PM Press T-shirt and a 50% discount on all purchases from our website.

Your Visa or Mastercard will be billed once a month, until you tell us to stop. Or until our efforts succeed in bringing the revolution around. Or the financial meltdown of Capital makes plastic redundant. Whichever comes first.

PM Press was founded at the end of
2007 by a small collection of folks with
decades of publishing, media, and organizing experience. PM Press co-con-
spirators have published and distributed
hundreds of books, pamphlets, CDs, and
DVDs. Members of PM have founded
enduring book fairs, spearheaded victorious tenant organizing campaigns,
and worked closely with bookstores, academic conferences, and even rock
band   We're
old   hat's
at s

We   oks,
par   and
insp   el
wit   an-
arch   k at
the   d
tim

PM   artists   roj-
ect